Walton Dorsey,
Wonder Boy

M A Field

WESTBOW°
PRESS
A DIVISION OF THOMAS NELSON
& ZONDERVAN

Scripture taken from the Holy Bible, NEW INTERNATIONAL VERSION®.
Copyright © 1973, 1978, 1984 by Biblica, Inc. All rights reserved worldwide.
Used by permission. NEW INTERNATIONAL VERSION® and NIV® are
registered trademarks of Biblica, Inc. Use of either trademark for the offering
of goods or services requires the prior written consent of Biblica US, Inc.

WestBow Press books may be ordered through booksellers or by contacting:

WestBow Press
A Division of Thomas Nelson & Zondervan
1663 Liberty Drive
Bloomington, IN 47403
www.westbowpress.com
1 (866) 928-1240

Because of the dynamic nature of the Internet, any web addresses or
links contained in this book may have changed since publication and
may no longer be valid. The views expressed in this work are solely those
of the author and do not necessarily reflect the views of the publisher,
and the publisher hereby disclaims any responsibility for them.

Any people depicted in stock imagery provided by Thinkstock are
models, and such images are being used for illustrative purposes only.
Certain stock imagery © Thinkstock.

This book is a work of fiction. All the characters portrayed in it are
fictitious, with the exception of Trevor Dearing. Any resemblance
of any of them to any actual living person is coincidental.

ISBN: 978-1-4908-6776-2 (sc)
ISBN: 978-1-4908-8241-3 (e)

Library of Congress Control Number: 2015901151

Print information available on the last page.

WestBow Press rev. date: 5/21/2015

Contents

CHAPTER 1

A teenage celebrity

Mrs Rita Dorsey had a strong desire to slam the door shut in the face of this blonde young woman who had announced herself as: "Corinne Carillon, Essex Today". However, her habitual self-control kicked in and she replied with a slight smile, "I'm sorry, he isn't here. You could try on Saturday; he may possibly be available then."

The TV reporter made an effort to subdue her frustration, responding with a wide smile: "Thanks for your help. Bye."

Today things had been relatively calm compared with yesterday, when the telephone had scarcely stopped ringing and she had continued to be pestered by half a dozen reporters from such national newspapers as *The World Today, The Daily News, UK Today* and *Scenes of Life*. Those with a better reputation such as *The Guardian* and *The Independent* had been considerate in arranging an interview and subsequently satisfied with the information they were given.

Mrs Dorsey wished her visitor a polite farewell and closed the front door thoughtfully, brushing her black curls away from her forehead. 'I hope Walton gets his homework done in time,' she said to herself. Then she ran back to the kitchen to finish preparing the stew for the family's evening meal.

"Who was that — anyone interesting?" queried her twelve-year-old daughter Esther casually, her blonde hair bobbing on her shoulders as she continued chopping up a turnip.

"Not really, an Essex Today reporter."

"Walton's getting to be quite a star, isn't he. I saw a paper in Miller's saying: 'WONDER BOY DOES IT AGAIN!' I hope he can cope with all the publicity. His meetings seem to have been in all the papers."

Their conversation was cut short by the ringing of the telephone on the kitchen wall. Seeing that her mother's hands were wet with juice from the onion she was cutting up, Esther picked up the phone. It was an ITV reporter.

"My brother isn't here at the moment," Esther told the caller, "can I take a message?"

"Tell them Saturday may be possible," said Mrs Dorsey.

"They want to know if I can tell them about the miracles," said Esther, looking at her mother for help.

Mrs Dorsey rinsed her hands and wiped them on a paper towel. "Maybe you can do the carrots?" she whispered quickly, reaching for the phone being extended towards her.

"Hallo, I'm Walton Dorsey's mother. I believe you would like to hear some details of the miracles that have been happening."

"Actually we want to interview your son. We understand he's 14 years old; is that correct?"

"Yes it is, but I'm afraid he isn't here right now. Shall I get him to call you back?"

"OK, my name is Kevin Anderson. Ask him to call me on 0845 801 3636."

Mrs Dorsey scribbled down the number on one of the pieces of paper she kept for the purpose on one of the open shelves on the wall, and put it in a separate section of the shelf. She and Esther had almost finished preparing the stew when her youngest son, seven-year-old Leo appeared, followed by his friend Peter.

"Can we have some orange juice please, Mum?"

"Alright, if Esther doesn't mind stirring the stew and turning the gas down low when it really bubbles up, I'll get you some," responded his mother, looking hopefully at Esther.

"OK, Mum. No problem," said Esther, taking the long-handled wooden spoon accordingly and stirring vigorously.

The two boys made themselves comfortable behind the kitchen table on the bench seat made by Mr Dorsey, to enjoy their drink, and were soon joined by Mum and Esther with a cup of tea and the biscuit barrel.

"Peter gets teased at school," Leo announced, "because his dad comes from Alsace-Lorraine. We were doing a project about dogs, and we learned that German shepherd dogs used to be called Alsatians, and some of the kids know where his dad comes from. Now they're saying his dad's an alsatian!" His dark eyes flashed with indignation.

"Tell them that's better than having a poodle as your dad!" retorted Esther with a smirk, eliciting chuckles and laughter all round.

"Does your dad speak French?" enquired Mrs Dorsey.

"Yes, he does a bit, but he mostly speaks German. He says he comes from Elsass-Lothringen, not Alsace-Lorraine."

"Oh, that area has been fought over all too often for centuries," said Mrs Dorsey with a sigh. "Sometimes part of Germany; sometimes part of France."

"Why do pandas like piano keyboards?" asked Leo in a challenging tone.

"Because they're black and white," answered Esther. "That's an old one."

"Why did the traffic jam?" Peter challenged.

"Because the lights were changing?" Leo suggested.

"No. Because they saw a zebra crossing!"

"Why did the fig roll?" came from Leo.

"Because it saw the apple turnover?" said Peter.

"Not this time," said Leo. "Because it saw the apple crumble!"

Further enlightenment was cut short by the phone ringing again. It was Walton. "Hi Mum. Some guys from the *Harlow Chronicle* want to interview me. I did a bit of my maths homework before coming out of school, and they were waiting for me. They're taking me to their offices to do the interview. I don't know what time I'll be back."

"OK, thanks for letting me know. See you later." She replaced the receiver with a growing feeling of uneasiness.

CHAPTER 2

Wild goose chase

Rita Dorsey went into the bathroom to pray. This was nothing unusual — it was the place where she often prayed; it was quiet and private. Although she had prayed early that morning for protection for each member of the family, she couldn't help feeling worried that Walton might be in some kind of danger. How could he be sure that the people he mentioned on the phone were really from the local paper?

Mr Robert Dorsey arrived home about a quarter past six, having cycled back from the train station. His work was in London with an engineering company which designed and produced steel turbine blades. He sometimes wondered why Harlow had to have such a lot of hills, even though Essex is generally a flat county.

"Phew!" he muttered as he came in through the back doorway, running a hand through his dark-blond hair, "it's warm work sometimes, riding a bike."

"Hallo Bob; but you do admit it's good exercise, don't you. Well, the weather's warming up at last — beginning to feel like nearly the end of June. Did you have to stand all the way?"

"No, not all the way today. Quite a few got out at Broxbourne, so I had a seat the rest of the way."

His wife arranged some decorative table mats and cutlery at appropriate place settings, followed by the huge steel French pressure cooker full of stew, consisting of lentils and various beans as well as the remains of yesterday's chicken, onions, turnips and carrots.

"Smells good!" remarked Mr Dorsey as he came back into the kitchen from the bathroom and was joined by Esther and Leo responding to their mother's shout: "Mangeing time!" (*Mange* pronounced the French way.)

"Where's Walton?" queried Dad.

"He said he was being taken to the *Harlow Chronicle* offices to be interviewed. They seem to be making a long session of it," said his wife, looking at her watch.

"Oh well, we may as well start without him. There'll probably be enough stew left for him when he does get back — if Leo doesn't eat it all!" Dad remarked with a grin.

"I admit I like stew," Leo responded with his own kind of grin, "but I'm not that much of a pig!"

"OK, let's pray," said his mother. Dad said a prayer of thanks to God for the food, and they were all soon enjoying and appreciating Mum's cooking.

Halfway through the meal the back door opened, and in walked Walton. He was what his friends called a "six-footer" — actually 6 foot 1 inch tall. His bushy hair was black like his mother's and his eyes were a striking dark brown. "Hi everyone," he said cheerfully, "any grub left? I'm starving!"

"We did save you a little bit," said Esther, "Leo didn't eat it all — he exercised self-control!"

A glance into the stewpot reassured her celebrity brother that it was still about half full, so he flopped onto a chair at the table.

"Those people at the *Harlow Chronicle* gave you a long interview, didn't they?" his mother commented as she filled his soup plate with stew.

"Well, as it happened — or didn't happen — they didn't actually interview me. I wondered where they were going. When we got to the end of Abercrombie Way, instead of going up to the town centre they turned right and went along First Avenue after the roundabout. I thought they must have some new offices over that way. But they kept going, and just mumbled something when I asked them where they were going. That turned out to be almost as far as Bishop's Stortford—"

"***What?!***" interjected his father incredulously.

"Well, then they started muttering something to each other and the driver turned into a side road, then turned the car round and brought me back to our school! They said there was no time for an interview, and they would contact me another time. So I've just walked back from school."

His parents were staring at each other, struggling to believe what they were hearing. Then his mother exclaimed, "Praise the Lord!"

"What for, specifically?" asked her husband, somewhat bewildered.

Mrs Dorsey explained how she had prayed for Walton's extra protection, because of her doubts about the authenticity of the "Harlow Chronicle reporters".

"D'you remember what the two guys looked like?" asked Esther.

"Erm… One had long ginger hair and a lot of freckles. The other one was really fat, and a skinhead. I didn't really notice what they were wearing … nothing very stylish, anyway. I was a bit surprised how dirty the car was inside…"

Now the telephone was tinkling again. Leo picked it up, as he was nearest. A frown developed as he listened. "Hold on a minute please," he said, then, whispering to his mother: "It's a Tracey Burton of the Harlow Chronicle wanting to speak to Walton."

His brother took the phone. "Walton Dorsey here."

"Hallo Walton. We'd like to arrange an interview with you as soon as possible. Would tomorrow be possible?"

"Well, if you're really serious about it," the boy celebrity replied, "I don't really have a lot of time to spare. I don't want a repetition of today's wild goose chase."

"I don't understand what you mean," responded the caller. "What wild goose chase?"

Walton gave her an account of his time-wasting trip almost to Bishop's Stortford and back.

"You refer to the two guys as my colleagues. Can you tell me what they looked like?"

Walton described them, adding, "They were driving a black Toyota Yaris, registration number B724 ZDW."

"None of my colleagues look anything like that," said Tracey. "We'll have to inform the police. Could you repeat that registration number please?"

When he did so she commented, "You obviously have an excellent memory!"

"Yes, I must admit it's good. I suppose you'll have to get the police involved," replied Walton. "I can come along to your offices in the town centre tomorrow after school if you like. About 4 o'clock?"

"4 o'clock will be fine, thanks. Bye."

"What about that ITV reporter, Mum?" said Esther. "You wrote down his number, didn't you."

"Oh yes; thanks for reminding me." She hurried to the shelf and passed the piece of paper to her son. "He wants you to call him about an interview," she said almost apologetically.

There was not much time left for Walton to do his French homework after he had finished talking to Kevin Anderson of ITV and the police. But as he enjoyed the subject and always had good grades in it, it took him only twenty minutes.

His alarm woke him at 6.15 next morning in good time to do his paper round. Leaving breakfast and a shower or wash till later, he hauled his bike out of the shed and cycled towards the newsagent's in the local shopping area.

With the bag of newspapers stowed on the back of his bike, he pedalled fast down one of the main roads towards his designated residential neighbourhood. He began to wonder why the car behind him was not overtaking him, even though there were no vehicles to be seen for at least 500 metres. As he turned into a side road leading to his delivery area he glanced back at the car behind. It was a black Toyota... He couldn't quite read the number plate, but it looked different from the number he had quoted to the *Harlow Chronicle* person and the police. 'They could have changed the number plate,' he mused. And as he rode on, he was disconcerted to see that the car had also turned into the same side road, travelling at about 15 m.p.h.

Walton sent up an "arrow prayer" for help and protection and pedalled faster. A quick glance back made him somewhat uneasy, for the driver, as far as he could make out, looked all too similar to the ginger-haired fellow of yesterday's abortive trip. Pedalling hard, he skirted a patch of what looked like the remains of a number of broken bottles lying on the road. He turned left at the next corner, dismounted after passing three houses and, deciding that there war no time to padlock the bike, he propped it up against a fence and ran up the path leading to the back garden of the nearest house. Stopping just past the rear corner of the house, he stood still and waited, listening.

CHAPTER 3

An early arrest

Walton could hear various noises which were developing into an unpleasant cacophony as he stood just inside the garden behind the semi-detached house where he had taken refuge: pop music and presenters' voices from different radio frequencies and several people shouting; a motor bike roaring past; a car's engine being revved up; the slamming of a door — probably a front door... then he heard the pleasant little melody of his mobile phone.

"Hallo?" he said cautiously.

"Police officer Jenkins here. Is that Walton Dorsey?"

"Yes it is. I'm trying to start my paper round in Mandela Croft..."

"We're probably not far from you, in Farringdon Road. We're holding two suspects in connection with your case. Can you come along to Farringdon Road to see if you're able to identify them?"

Walton cycled fast back into the road he had turned out of, to be greeted by the sight of the black Toyota behind a police car, where two men, their arms being held by two policemen, were standing, wearing handcuffs.

As he came closer, he recognised the two men as the pair who had fraudulently claimed to be from the *Harlow Chronicle*. Then he noticed that the Toyota was tilted forward; its two front tyres were completely flat.

A tall police officer introduced himself as Richard Jenkins. When Walton confirmed their suspicions about the identity of the men, Jenkins added, "Their car tyres must be extremely thin — illegally thin in fact — otherwise that broken glass probably wouldn't have punctured them that quickly." He thanked Walton for his help, agreed that the boy could give his statement at the police station after school, and the criminals were bundled into the police car.

It was almost 8 o'clock when Walton arrived home. The bathroom was now occupied by Esther, so he helped himself to his favourite cereal and made a pot of tea. His mother had already left in her Rover car to attend to the elderly patients she looked after three days a week as a nursing carer. Dad had also gone to work, cycling to the train station.

Leo appeared in the kitchen as he was pouring himself a second cup of tea. "Any Malted Oatflakes left?" he queried.

Walton shook the packet that he had left on the table. "It feels like it," he said, aware that it was about three-quarters full, "try to leave some for tomorrow!"

Reassured by his brother's smile, Leo filled a bowl with cereal and went to get the milk out of the fridge.

"Oops!" The half-full bottle of milk slipped out of his grasp and shattered on the tiled floor, the milk splashing in all directions. "Oh-oh-ooh," he wailed, struggling to fight off the tears.

"Never mind, Leo," said his brother soothingly, "you know what they say: it's no use crying over spilt milk. Let's get the mop and mop it up." He strode into the small utility room, found the mop and had soon got rid of most of the milk. "It's OK, I'll deal with the glass," he said, carefully picking out the larger pieces, which he put into a discarded freezer bag he had extricated from the kitchen waste bin. "Can you find an old newspaper?"

His small brother soon found one in the waste paper recycling collection, and Walton was able to use it to get rid of all the remaining little fragments of glass.

Now Esther came into the kitchen for her breakfast. Walton glanced at his watch. "8.30!" he exclaimed, running out of the room and up the stairs to the bathroom.

"Did something get broken?" Esther enquired as she found herself a cereal bowl.

"Yeah," Leo replied. "I dropped a bottle of milk. It was darn slippery!"

Esther looked around the floor. "Well, someone seems to have done a good job of cleaning up the mess," she commented.

"Walton did it for me. Mum had already gone to work."

"That was kind of him. I hope it doesn't make him late for school." A further thought occurred to her: "If we had our milk in plastic bottles like they have in Harrison's, they wouldn't break if we dropped them," she observed, helping herself to cereal.

"Mum says the milk we get from the farmer is better than supermarket milk," said Leo.

"I expect that's true," his sister conceded. "Maybe it's cheaper for the farmer to use glass bottles."

Walton got to school a few minutes to nine, having had a quick shower and cycled to school. Normally he preferred to walk home with his friends, when possible. Gareth and Ollie were good fun.

On Monday morning at break time the friends met up after managing at length to get away from the classmates and others who shouted, "Three cheers for the Wonder Boy!" Some of them had relatives who had been healed at Walton's meetings, and they were crowding around their own TV star, chattering excitedly about how good he had looked in his interviews ....

Gareth seemed to be bursting with news. "Hey, Walt, there's a lot of twittering going on about you. Some people thought your interviews on TV were nang, but some are pretty annoyed — they don't seem to like what you said about gays."

"Some of them are threatening you," added Ollie, "like: 'If you don't stop this homophobic garbage, we'll get you!'"

Walton replied, "Some of what I said was quoting the Bible: Leviticus Chapter 18 verse 22. I didn't even mention Chapter 20, verse 13. Weren't they interested in the miracles? Like that student who was healed of the tropical disease that was killing her and none of the specialists could do anything about?"

"No, they were only interested in the other stuff," said Ollie, stopping a football with his foot and giving it a kick past Gareth, who zoomed after it, and they were soon enjoying a bit of footie.

By Tuesday, which had become the weekly evening of "Praise and Healing" at Kingsmount Community Church, the church was already half full at 6 o'clock although the meeting was not due to begin till 7.00 pm. The *Harlow Chronicle*, published on Friday, had given Walton's interview the front page, and the TV interviews had created a stir locally as well as nationally. At 6.45 the stewards were placing extra chairs down the centre aisle and at the sides. There was a low stage at one end of the hall, where the musicians usually sat. Chairs were also placed here, leaving only a relatively small space free. By 7 o'clock people were sitting on the window sills, and there was simply no other space for any more. A blackboard was brought from the pastor's house, and this was set up near the main door with the message: CHURCH FULL — COME BACK EARLY NEXT WEEK.

The meeting started with singing accompanied by two guitarists, a pianist, a drummer and a girl playing the flute. Most of the songs had a good, swinging rhythm and a lot of the people included clapping with their singing.

The pastor, Rev. Rolf Robnott, then read out some letters and emails. "This one is from Janice Thornton, a photographer who lives in Kent and specialises in children's photographs. She writes: 'I would like to express my sincere thanks to Walton Dorsey for his part in my healing. I was diagnosed as having a brain tumour about a year ago, but after Walton prayed for me 6 weeks ago the doctors now say they can find no trace of the tumour or any cancer in my head or my body.'" Other letters and messages similarly thanked Walton for helping in the healing of arthritis, gallstones, a stomach ulcer, and spondylitis.

After another couple of songs Pastor Robnott gave a twenty-minute talk about faith. He pointed out that you exercise a kind of faith whenever you board an aircraft. You have faith that the plane is going to carry you to the place you want to go, otherwise you wouldn't get on it. He challenged his listeners to put their faith in Jesus Christ, who is alive in the heavenly dimension and has the power to help us in every situation. Pastor Robnott had a way of speaking that held everyone's attention. Apart from his voice there was absolute silence, even though there were about 400 people seated there.

When he had finished speaking it was Walton's turn to go to the microphone standing at the front. He gave a flashing smile at the people sitting in the first few rows, and introduced himself, looking more like a 17- or 18-year-old than a boy of 14. He explained how he had become a Christian at the age of 12 through visiting Trevor Dearing's meetings at Hainault, also in Essex, like Harlow. He had become aware of the presence of Jesus at those meetings, and what Trevor Dearing said made sense. Walton told them that his mother's eyes had been healed. She had been extremely short-sighted, but Rev. Dearing prayed for her eyes, in the name of Jesus, placing his hand gently over them. From that time on, she had not needed glasses.

"You may have seen me being interviewed on TV," the tall schoolboy continued, "so you will have heard that Jesus uses me as a channel for his healing love. If you need healing of any kind — physical or psychological or emotional, just come forward. A steward will stand behind you, because some people feel so light when the Holy Spirit blesses them that they fall down onto the floor. They don't hurt themselves," he added with a smile, "but the steward will gently lower you to the floor if you start to fall."

A line of people was already forming in front of Walton as he said the last few words. He began to pray for each one. After about a dozen people had been prayed for with Walton's hands placed usually on their heads, but sometimes over a painful area, a woman in a wheelchair approached. She told the unusually compassionate schoolboy that she had MS.

The congregation had been singing softly in the meantime, but now Walton held up his hand for quietness. "This lady whose name is Gillian has MS," he said. "If you believe that Jesus is able to heal MS, please raise your hand."

Just over half the people did so. "Those of you who raised your hand please join with me in praying for Gillian now." He prayed in a powerful way, with one hand on Gillian's head and the other lifted up to receive the healing power.

"Wow!" Gillian exclaimed a few moments later. "Something warm went right through me." She waved her arms about; then she began to move her legs up and down as she sat there in the wheelchair. Suddenly she said excitedly: "I'm going to try walking!"

And she did just that. She got up out of the wheelchair and walked to the side of the church; then she turned round, straightened up a bit more, and walked back, past Walton to the other side of the hall.

"Praise the Lord!" Walton declared exultantly. "Let's give Jesus a clap offering." Everyone clapped with enthusiasm, many with upraised arms. "Thank You, Jesus," said Walton. "Thank You for being here with us. Please continue to pour out Your healing love on all the people gathered here, seeking healing."

He then beckoned to the next person in the line to come forward, and the healing ministry resumed. There were several instances of sticks and crutches being discarded, but probably more impressive was the case of the young man, who looked to be about 25 years old, who suddenly cried out loudly after prayer: "I can hear! I can hear everything loud and clear!" He told Walton, who relayed the information to the congregation, that he had been profoundly deaf since he was a toddler, and none of his hearing aids had been really effective.

"Oh-h-h — it's wonderful!!" he enthused.

"Jesus is wonderful," Walton responded; "let's sing, 'Praise him on the trumpet'. This was a lively, bouncy song that encouraged a good number to get up and dance around wherever there was a bit of space.

At 10 o'clock it was announced that Walton would be available in a small room for 15 minutes if anyone had any special need for prayer. But the meeting would continue until 11 o'clock for those who wanted to stay. A few people left, and at 10.15 Walton went out by a rear door to make his way home.

It was only a 15-minute walk to their home at 99, Primrose Park. The weather had turned chilly, but he was happy to see some stars, in spite of the urban street lights. His thoughts turned to the two guys who had apparently wanted to kidnap him. 'The police probably won't be able to hold them,' he thought. 'They didn't actually do anything criminal — except for having illegal car tyres; maybe they'll keep them locked up for a while till they can be put on trial for that.'

He didn't see any pedestrians as he turned into the road leading to Primrose Park.

CHAPTER 4

The Adrian Carter Show

Assuming that Leo and probably Esther had gone to bed, Walton let himself in through the front door quietly, using his key. His parents had just finished watching the ten o'clock news, so Mr Dorsey turned the volume down when his son strolled in. "You're back in good time," he commented. "How did it go this evening?"

"Great! There was a woman with MS in a wheelchair, and she got up and walked across from one side of the church to the other after I prayed!"

His mother gasped: "Wow! She must have had it for a long time, if she was in a wheelchair!"

"Well, don't forget how a leper was healed instantaneously by Jesus. Sometimes it happens straight away; sometimes the healing is gradual," said Walton, disappearing into the kitchen, where he got a cup out of the dishwasher. He filled it with milk and placed it in the microwave for a drink of hot chocolate.

"Did you say Friday evening you're going to be on the Adrian Carter Show?" queried his mother. "It would be difficult for me to be ready in time to drive you there..."

"He could meet me at Liverpool Street station," suggested Mr Dorsey. "What time do they want you there?"

"7 o'clock."

"Maybe you could get permission to miss your last lesson. Then we could have a bite to eat before going on to the TV studio," his father proposed.

Walton finished his bedtime drink. "Probably," he agreed, "it's double art, so it should be alright." His art teacher was an attractive young woman of 23, with long blonde hair. The way she sometimes looked at him reminded him of his grandmother's spaniel. She probably wouldn't object to him missing a lesson.

THE ADRIAN CARTER SHOW

Adrian Carter: Well, Walton, they're calling you the Wonder Boy. What do you think of that?

Walton Dorsey: Not much. It isn't me who does the healing — it's Jesus.

AC: Well, maybe we'll come back to that in a couple of minutes. First let me say you don't look like a 14-year-old schoolboy, even if you are wearing school uniform.

WD: Maybe I should've brought my birth certificate!

AC: Well, you must admit it's unusual for a 14-year-old to be so tall.

WD: There happen to be quite a lot of tall people in our family. My father's 3 inches taller than me, and my brother is exactly 6 foot 8 — at least, he was at the last count. He's probably still growing. He's 18.

AC: OK, let's go back to the subject of healing miracles. What makes you so sure it's Jesus who produces these healings?

WD: The fact that I ask him to do it. The Bible tells us that he said, "If you ask anything in my name, I will do it." Jesus is alive, and in a position of power in the dimension of heaven.

AC: What makes you think he's alive?

WD: He came back to life after being crucified and put in a tomb. The cloths his body had been wrapped in were lying on the floor of the tomb, with the head cloth folded up separately. If the disciples or anyone else had managed to steal the body, they would have been in too much of a hurry to unwrap it first!

AC: How long have you been a Christian?

WD: About 2 years. I started going to Sunday School when I was about 3, but it didn't all fall into place till I was 12, at a Trevor Dearing meeting when he came to our church. I really understood why the Son of God had let Himself be crucified, taking the penalty for our sins upon Himself. Then about 6 months ago I was at another of Trevor Dearing's meetings and he prayed for me to be baptised in the Holy Spirit.

AC: I thought being baptised involves water, doesn't it?

WD: Yes, but this means being immersed in, or filled with the Holy Spirit, who is God in a different form. He gives people spiritual gifts, and one of them is healing.

AC: What about all the people in NHS hospitals — why don't you visit them and heal all of them?

WD: Perhaps you should ask the hospital chaplains why they don't do so.

AC: How many people have been healed so far at your meetings?

WD: I don't know. We've received a lot of letters and emails from people wanting to say thank you for my part in their healing. I haven't counted them.

AC: What about politics? Do you think Christians should be involved in politics?

WD: Yes, I do. Politics is about organising resources and making laws for the good of all the people, and the Christian faith is basically: love God and love your neighbour. We need politicians who manage things so that the wealthy contribute more to the common good than those on low incomes. That way there would be more of a sense of fairness. I think things like water, gas and electricity should be nationalised, because everyone needs them; there shouldn't be a profit motive involved, or shareholders pushing the price up unnecessarily. There would still be opportunities to help each other.

AC: Is there any special advice you would give to politicians?

WD: I'd prefer to give some advice to millionaires and billionaires and multimillionaires: Half of the world's wealth is owned by just 85 people. Give away 90% of your money if you're a billionaire or a multimillionaire, and a large percentage if you're a millionaire. You could do so much good, and in most cases you'd just be giving it back to the people who produced it by their hard work!

AC: What do you think of same-sex marriage?

WD: It's a very bad idea. Firstly because homosexual practice is prohibited by God — check it out in Leviticus Chapter 18 verse 22, where it says to men: "Do not lie with a man as with a woman; that is detestable", and in Leviticus 20 verse 13 it says that those who do so should suffer the death penalty. Secondly, marriage was ordained by God to be between one man and one woman.

AC: Do you think practising homosexuals and lesbians should be put to death?

WD: We're not under the old covenant any more; we're under the New Covenant, which means there's forgiveness available for every kind of sin through the death of Jesus on the cross.

AC: Don't you think gay people should have equal rights?

WD: A lot of harm has been done by overdoing the idea of equality. Especially with regard to homosexuals. Only a minute percentage of the population are born with an innate tendency to be homosexual or are psychologically inclined that way from infancy. But in this day and age the vast majority of practising homosexual people have been corrupted into behaving that way, and most of them claim that it's in their genes, so they can't help it. Quite a lot come from broken homes; a lot of them were abused as children, and others went along with what their friends were doing as teenagers. So because of the general attitude that has been promoted in the name of equality, they think that's the way they are, and that's the way they have to remain — so they miss out on having a loving wife in the way God intended, and having children. The apostle Paul calls it a perversion. When it applies to women becoming lesbians, I think it's even more of a perversion — a kind of mutual self-gratification. Governments that ban the promotion of homosexuality to teenagers and younger children are right. Our gov—

Cyril Cambit gave vent to a string of obscenities as he switched off the TV set furiously. Glaring at his friend and flat-mate Jeff, he snarled, "What's the idea of listenin' to that garbage? I thought you was watchin' somethink interestin'."

"I wanted to 'ear what this kid 'ad to say," said Jeff, getting himself another can of beer.

"We 'eard 'im the other night — it's all the same ol' Scotch mist. I'm the boss 'ere—"

"Yeah, don' I know it! Anyway, there was a woman on telly yesterday w'o said she'd been healed by this boy of MS. She'd 'ad it for 10 years."

"What's MS?"

"Multiple sclerosis. I think it affects all the muscles, so they can't do anything much except sit in a wheelchair."

"Maybe, but 'e should shut 'is gob about guys like us. When are we g'nna teach 'im a lesson?"

"We'll 'ave to find out what Tom and the others wanna do."

"Yeah, I'll give 'im a shout." He unlocked his mobile phone and jabbed viciously at Contacts.

CHAPTER 5

Merle

On Monday morning Walton debated with himself as he went from house to house on his paper round, whether he should share with his friend Ollie Patel the vision he had seen as he woke up that morning. He was in little doubt about the details, but could he be sure that it was a form of "word of knowledge"? 'This may be one of the gifts of the Holy Spirit,' he said to himself, 'or it may not.' He was in a quandary: should he try to get a message to Ollie's dad or should he say nothing?

By break time, having prayed about it, Walton was 90% sure it was a valid word of knowledge.

"Hi Walt," Ollie greeted him, with a look of indignation as he continued: "That scumbag Monty Banston is telling everybody you're a con-man, and all the so-called miracles are a put-up job!"

Walton stared at his friend for a moment, then he replied, "What about Phoebe Sanderson's mother? A lot of people knew how ill she was before I prayed for her. And there are a whole lot of other kids in this school whose relatives have been healed at the Tuesday night meetings. They know their relatives were definitely ill, right enough!"

"Yeah, he's on a losing streak trying to spread manky rumours."

"Ollie," Walton said seriously to his friend, trying to ignore the 10% doubtfulness about his vision, "did you say your dad would be flying to Indonesia today?"

"That's right; he's got to meet some people in Jakarta on business."

"You'll have to call him and tell him not to go today."

"What are you talking about? I don't know what time his flight is s'posed to be. Why shouldn't he go today?"

"I had a kind of vision this morning. I saw your dad at the airport, then I saw a Boeing 747 coming down into the sea about 2 or 3 miles from Jakarta! See if you can contact him. Get him to rebook on a flight for tomorrow!"

When Mr James Patel heard what his son had to say, he just wanted to pour scorn on the idea of Walton's "vision". "It was most likely just a dream," he said. "I don't think I should worry about it."

Seeing Ollie shaking his head in his direction, Walton seized the phone and insisted, "**Please**, Mr Patel, I'm almost certain it's a warning from God. **Please** change your flight to tomorrow. Better safe than sorry!"

"Alright Walton. I'll think about it. Thanks for trying to help. Bye."

"I hope he does rebook his flight," said Ollie anxiously as he stowed his mobile away in his school bag.

It was after they had finished their school lunch together and Walton, Ollie and Gareth were considering whether to go outside or amuse themselves in the indoor games hall, when Ollie heard the jingle of his mobile.

"Dad here. Thought you'd like to know that I told the people in Jakarta that I couldn't make it till Wednesday. I managed to rebook OK. Tell Walton I agree with him — better safe than sorry. Tell your mum I'm staying here in a hotel tonight and I'll call her later. Bye."

After school Walton ran out through a rear door to the cycle shed in an attempt to evade the classmates of both genders who wanted to claim him as their friend, then met up with Gareth and Ollie along the road.

"Hi there, Wonder Boy!" Gareth teased, "done any good miracles lately?"

"No, but I know someone who did, not long ago — but he wouldn't claim to have done it himself. It involved a key."

Walton's two friends were intrigued. They were by now getting used to the idea of people being miraculously healed of various illnesses and disabilities; but a key? That was something else.

"It happened after one of Trevor Dearing's meetings at Hainault. He told us about it the following week. A woman came to him for help because she had lost her car keys, so she couldn't drive home. Trevor asked her if she had any other kind of key.

"'Only my Yale front-door key,' she said. Then Trevor prayed for the gift of miracles, which is also one of the gifts of the Holy Spirit, and he prayed to be able to use the Yale key in the ignition. He was able to fit it in, and the woman was able to drive home! Next morning her husband tried to put the front-door key in the ignition, but it was impossible."

"Wow! That really was a miracle!" exclaimed Ollie. Gareth agreed.

After a few minutes reflecting on the impossible having become possible, Ollie remarked, "Wouldn't it be great to have a key that would fit into any lock! One key to open any door!"

"Or any cupboard," suggested Gareth, "like Charlie's locker, to put a frog in it!"

"Or a bank vault..." added Ollie.

"Don't forget Trevor Dearing **prayed** about the woman's key," Walton reminded them.

"The money could be used to help the poor," said Gareth.

"Tell that to the billionaires!" retorted Walton.

The three friends continued ambling their way home with their usual good-natured banter. "How d'you spell 'hungry horse' using only four letters?" asked Gareth.

"Starvin' Marvin," said Ollie.

"Back to school with you and learn how to count!" said Walton.

"The answer is... MTGG!" Gareth announced, dodging a friendly fist from Ollie.

"How many pages long is the world's highest prime number so far?" came from Walton.

"500?" guessed Ollie.

"A thousand?" Gareth suggested.

"Both wrong! The answer is 5,000!" declared Walton.

"Wow!" responded Ollie, "5,000 *pages!!*"

"My Great-uncle Alfred told me about an interesting puzzle," said Gareth. "He worked in the central post office in London, and some of the time his job was to decipher addresses on letters that the postman couldn't read or understand."

"Interesting," commented Walton.

"Yeah. Well one day he was given a letter from somewhere in Africa addressed to someone in England, giving the town as: Has Bedella Such. How should it have been spelt?"

His two friends cogitated for a while, but finally had to admit defeat.

"The answer is... Ashby-de-la-Zouch!"

"Never heard of it," said Walton.

"Nor have I," said Ollie. "Whereabouts in England is it — sounds a bit French."

"I hadn't heard of it either till my great-uncle told me about it. It's about 20 miles north-east of Birmingham."

"Did your great-uncle come up with the solution?" queried Walton.

"I think so, but it may have been his wife. She was always doing crosswords."

"How does the man in the moon get his hair cut?" asked Ollie.

His two friends thought for a few moments, then gave up.

"Eclipse it!" declared Ollie triumphantly. And so it went on until Walton's melodious mobile broke in on it.

"Is that Walton Dorsey?"

"Who's speaking?"

"It's Matt Pearson, one of your father's colleagues at Walker's Turbines."

"Hi. Is Dad alright?"

"No, I'm afraid not. He had an attack of food poisoning, and they've taken him into Bart's Hospital. He's in intensive care."

"Thanks for letting us know. Weren't you able to contact my mother?"

"No. The number we tried was unobtainable."

"OK, I'll let her know as soon as possible. Thanks again. Bye."

Walton decided, however, to wait until he had phoned the hospital before relaying the message to his mother. "I'll have a time of quietness and prayer when I get home," he told his friends.

There was no sign of Esther or Leo when he arrived home, so he concluded they had gone to their friends' houses. He went upstairs into what was really his brother Nathan's room, but while he was away at Nottingham University Walton used it to do his homework and otherwise use the computer. His own room he shared with Leo, who was taking a long time to learn to organise his toys and other belongings. Esther's room was extremely small — just a box room, but the bed which her father had made was long enough and comfortable enough. She had a small dressing-table and a good-sized cupboard, so she had no complaints.

In response to Walton's enquiry when he called the hospital it was confirmed that his father was in intensive care. He had eaten something contaminated with a dangerous e-coli bug; he was "stable but rather poorly".

Walton knew that God was able to heal in response to prayer, whether the laying-on of hands was used or not. He reminded himself of the instances in the New Testament when Jesus healed sick people some distance away.

After praying he felt better, and made the call to his mother. On hearing the news she said, "I'm with a very frail elderly man at the moment. He has a bit of dementia, and needs various things done for him before I leave. I'm sure you've already prayed for Dad, haven't you?" When her son replied in the affirmative she said, "I may be able to get away a bit earlier than usual, but can't promise. See you later."

While he was doing his English homework, involving writing a précis of a really boring speech apparently by a politician, he heard someone come in via the front door.

"Hi, Esther. What are you having to drink?"

"I'm just putting the kettle on for a cup of tea. Would you like one?"

Walton accepted her offer gratefully. He had decided not to tell his sister and young brother about what had happened to Dad until their mother had come home and they could all pray for him together.

"Is Leo playing with his friends?" he asked. Usually his younger brother waited at school for Esther, but sometimes he went home with a friend.

"Yes, Miss Baker said he had gone home with Harry."

"Have you got much homework?"

"Quite a bit; the German probably won't take long, but the history will take forever I expect."

"Well, I'll leave you to it then. I'll go and get on with my English."

Walton had almost finished his précis when his mother arrived home, so he finished it off and went downstairs.

"Hi, Mum. I haven't told Esther or Leo yet about Dad. I thought it would be best to wait till you came home, so that we could all pray together."

"Good thinking, Walton. Let's get together in the living-room."

Leo had returned in the meantime from Harry's house, so they settled down to pray. Mrs Dorsey had just begun to pray, however, when the telephone on the wall chirruped obtrusively.

It was a Sister at St Bartholomew's Hospital. "Is that Mrs Dorsey?"

"Yes, it is. How…"

"Hallo dear, I'm feeling fine now, thank the Lord!"

"**Oh!** Bob! You're better already! We had just started to pray for you!"

"Well you can say thank You to God instead. I expect you prayed for me earlier, didn't you?"

"Yes, I did, and so did Walton, but we wanted to pray as a family. Praise the Lord!"

The following day the news media had a new story around lunchtime. It was reported that a Boeing 747 heading for Jakarta had come down into the sea about 3 miles from Jakarta. It was not known how many survivors had been picked up, and the cause of the accident was unknown.

Walton, Ollie and Gareth were on their way home from school when Ollie's mobile interrupted their usual banter. It was his father.

"Hallo Ollie, have you heard the news?"

When his son replied in the negative, Mr Patel sounded as if he was struggling to control his emotions. "Walton was right! It's been on the news that a Boeing 747 **did** crash into the sea near Jakarta! It's the one I was scheduled to be on…"

Ollie cut in with a mix of incredulity and astonishment: "Whough! Let me tell Wa—"

"Tell him I can never thank him enough for persuading me to rebook the flight! Must go now; bye."

When Ollie relayed the news to Walton, the three friends remained rooted to the spot, wide-eyed and open mouthed. Then Walton, looking thoughtful, commented: "It's a relief to know that I didn't mess up your dad's plans unnecessarily; it confirms to me that it was a warning from God. But I realise now that I should have prayed for the plane and the people on it. I don't know why I didn't."

"Nobody's perfect," said Gareth cheerfully. "Let's have a jog home."

Rita Dorsey went into the bathroom to pray. In chats with two of her friends she had heard that more threats were being posted against Walton. She pondered the fact that he often walked home alone after the Tuesday evening meetings.

"Heavenly Father," she whispered, "if Walton is in any special danger today or this evening, please put your angel(s) in charge of him, so that no harm of any kind can happen to him or be done to him." She visualised the word 'angel' with the letter 's' in brackets, because she didn't know how many angels God would want to use to protect her son from any possible attack. "Thank You Lord," she added.

The Tuesday evening meeting was as lively and charged with spiritual excitement as ever, although there were not so many people present. The extra chairs down the aisles had been declared too risky in case of fire, and no one was allowed to sit on the window sills.

About 20 minutes into the healing ministry time, there was a sudden shout: "I can see! Ohhh! I can see everything!"

Amid a buzz of excitement throughout the church hall Walton led the woman to the microphone. "How long have you been blind?" he asked.

"Since I was seven," she replied, pushing back her blonde hair, and continuing to stare around in wonder at all the people.

"May I ask how old you are now?"

"Thirty-two. Ohh, it's marvellous! Wonderful to be able to see again!"

After a clap offering of thanks and a thank You song, the healing ministry resumed. But Walton was finding it difficult to concentrate. He had become aware of a girl with the most beautiful long deep red-auburn hair sitting in the third row from the front. He thought she was the most beautiful girl he had ever seen — whether in reality or on the screen. How could he control his thoughts? 'Maybe if we sing something really meaningful,' he thought.

"Let's sing 'My Song is Love Unknown," he announced. "It's number 402."

As the voices of the people united in singing the words, Walton's self-control returned and he was able to join in singing:

My song is love unknwn:
My Saviour's love to me –
Love to the loveless shown, that they might lovely be.
Oh who am I, that for my sake
My Lord should take frail flesh and die?

He came from his blessed throne
Salvation to bestow
But men made strange and few
The longed-for Christ would own.
But oh, my Friend! My Friend indeed
Who at my need his life did spend.

Sometimes they strew his way,
And his sweet praises sing,
Resounding all the day Hosannas to their King;
Then "Crucify!" is all their breath,
And for his death they thirst and cry.

Why, what has my Lord done?
What makes this rage and spite?
He made the lame to walk, He gave the blind their sight.
Sweet injuries! Yet they for these
Do bring false pleas and 'gainst him rise.

They rise and needs must have
My dear Lord made away;
A murderer they save
The Prince of life they slay.

Yet willing He to suffering goes,
That He his foes from thence might free.

Here might I stay and sing no story so Divine!
Never was love, dear King, never was grief like Thine.
This is my Friend, in whose sweet praise
I all my days could gladly spend!

At 10 o'clock Walton withdrew to his counselling room, and was almost overwhelmed with the fabulously pleasurable shock of finding that amazingly attractive girl waiting to speak to him!

"Hi, I'm Merle O'Brien," she began.

"I'm sorry, I only counsel males; the female counselling room is along there," said Walton, rapidly regaining his composure and pointing along the corridor. "But I'd be delighted to talk to you sometime. How about Saturday? Would you like to join me for a lunchtime pizza at the Pizza Place?"

"That sounds very nice. Yes, I'd like that. What time?"

"Shall we say 12.15? It can get quite crowded on a Saturday, but if we're early enough it should be OK."

"Yes, alright. See you on Saturday."

Walton watched her make her way to the other counselling room, and waved as she found the appropriate door. He felt somewhat dazed. Wow!

He could think of little else as he walked home from the church, only Merle. As usual there was not much traffic on the roads at this time, and hardly any pedestrians. After crossing the main road into the road leading to Primrose Park, he didn't pay any attention to a minibus which turned into this road and came to a stop almost opposite where he was walking.

Cyril Cambit and his five cronies had been following Walton at a good distance behind, from his leaving the church. "OK, out now!" he shouted, and they all jumped out onto the pavement. But there they stopped, unable to believe their eyes. Two tall, muscular men had suddenly appeared, as if out of nowhere — one each side of Walton, and were walking with him. They were at least 20cm taller than the boy.

"Where'd those two guys come from? They wasn't there a minute ago!" growled Cyril, trying to whisper.

"I didnae see 'em," said one of the group named Jock.

"Nor did I," said Stan.

"Looks like one of 'em 's got a sword," said Tom.

"The other one's got somethin' as well, maybe a different sort o' sword," said Dino.

"I wouldn't wanna get too close to 'em," said Alf.

Walton chatted politely to the two friendly men who had come alongside him as they turned the corner into Primrose Park. When they reached the smaller road leading to Walton's house, the two men stopped. One of them said, "It's been nice to talk to you. Maybe we'll see you again sometime. Bye." They remained standing there until Walton reached his front door. As he inserted his key in the lock, he turned to wave; but they had gone.

CHAPTER 6

A deadly threat

Cyril Cambit and his band of would-be punitive warriors settled themselves back on the seats of the minibus, trying to find an explanation for the sudden appearance of the two men.

"Maybe they came from one o' the houses," suggested Tom.

"There isnae a house near there," said Jock, "only a fence."

"They could've jumped over it," said Dino.

"Nah," said Stan, "that kind o' stockade panel fencin' is usually 2 metres high. Maybe they'd been joggin', or in trainin' for a race."

"Well, whatever. Hey Cyril, why don't we stop off at the Small Copper for a couple o' beers?" Alf proposed.

"Yeah, let's do that," Cyril agreed. He turned the minibus and headed towards the northern part of the town. "We'll get 'im some other time."

Meanwhile, Cyril's flat-mate Jeff had been watching the Adrian Carter interview with Walton Dorsey on his tablet. He had declined to go with Cyril and the others, saying that he wanted to watch TV. He watched the Adrian Carter Show again from the beginning, because he found it really interesting, especially when the boy talked about Jesus coming back to life after dying on the cross. 'What if he really is alive in a different dimension, and can communicate with us?' he wondered. 'I seem to remember from Sunday School that he worked a lot of miracles… Let's see what else this kid had to say.' He located the next part of the interview:

Adrian Carter: What about Muslims? Are they equal to Christians?

Walton Dorsey: It's not about equality. We're all basically equal in the sight of God. But Muslims don't believe the same things Christians do. The Koran gives a different view of God from the way the Bible presents Him. There was a Muslim young woman who wanted to worship God in the way He wants, but she was puzzled by the important differences in the two books. So one night she placed a copy of the Bible next to the Koran and prayed that God would tell her which one she should live by. The answer came: "The one in which I am called 'Father'." So she became a Christian. The title of the book she wrote was: *I Dared to Call Him Father*.

AC: Are there any other differences?

WD: Oh yes, quite a lot. I think Mohammed was misled by the Middle Eastern Christians in the 7th Century who called Mary, the mother of Jesus, the "Queen of Heaven". He had the impression that they worshipped three gods, and he saw it as his mission to teach Arabs that there is only one God. He doesn't seem to have heard of the Trinity: one God in three Persons, Father, Son and Holy Spirit, like water, ice and steam.

AC: What sort of career would you like?

WD: Probably a Christian minister, but I'd like to do physics and biochemistry at Uni, as well as theology. The more scientists discover about God's creation, the more I admire Him.

AC: Which football team do you support?

WD: None of them. I like playing football, but I don't watch other people doing so. There are a lot more interesting things to do, and only a finite number of hours available.

AC: Well, talking of time is a useful note to bring our conversation to an end. Thank you, Walton.

Jeff Yardley switched off his tablet. He continued to sit there in his club chair, pondering over what he had heard. That book, *I Dared to Call Him Father*, sounded interesting. Maybe he could get one on the Internet. His own father had gone off and left his mother with 3 children when he was about 6. 'I don't think God is much like my dad,' he reflected. 'Christians seem to think He's a lot better.' He decided that he would definitely try to get hold of a copy of the book.

He had also developed a deep respect for this schoolboy who could apparently work miracles. The church where the miracles seemed to happen was on the other side of town. 'I s'pose I could get there by bus,' he thought.

Merle O'Brien struggled to concentrate on the history homework she was expected to do by tomorrow. How could she, when all she could think about was yesterday evening at Kingsmount Community Church, and meeting Walton Dorsey! He had seemed quite pleased to talk to her, even though she had gone to the wrong counselling room. 'I hope he was serious about meeting up for lunch at the Pizza Place,' she mused. 'I wonder if he'll have time afterwards for us to get to know each other...' Her computer had now come up with a massive amount of detail regarding the Chartists, so she made a huge effort to stop thinking about Walton, and pick out appropriate points that would help to answer the question.

It continued to be difficult, however. The news media were continually reminding her of him. Ollie's father, James Patel, had passed on the news to the media that Walton Dorsey had warned him against flying to Jakarta that particular day, so he had rebooked the flight. The news items proclaimed: 'Wonder Boy Walton Dorsey saves his friend's father's life', 'Walton Dorsey predicts plane disaster'.

Then there was the news of Gemma Jacobson, the blind woman who had regained her sight at Walton Dorsey's latest Tuesday night meeting. Merle's computer flashed up quotes from some of the tabloid newspapers: "WONDER BOY DOES WONDERS!", "BLIND GEMMA CAN SEE, THANKS TO WONDER BOY!"

Merle printed out several pages of info that could be useful, and switched off her computer. The history teacher preferred assignments to be computer-written or typed, but Merle decided that she would have to give an excuse about having problems with her computer. She assembled some ideas in pencil, then wrote her answer in ink.

Three days later — days which had dragged interminably — she was at the Pizza Place in the town centre. She stood near the entrance for a few minutes, wondering whether to go inside, when suddenly a tall young fellow wearing a baseball cap and sunglasses came striding up to her, taking off the cap to reveal his bushy black hair, and removing his sunglasses.

"Oh!" gasped Merle, "I didn't recognise you!"

"That was the intention," he responded with a grin, replacing the cap and sunglasses, grasping her elbow and ushering her into the restaurant. "And hopefully not too many people in here will recognise me."

Seated at a table for two near a window, Walton pushed the cap loosely over his hair and passed a menu to this girl whose beauty seemed even enhanced by the addition of sunlight to the restaurant's artificial lighting.

"So, Merle — I like your name; it means 'blackbird' in French, doesn't it. The English word doesn't do justice to the bird, especially when it sings. It sounds better in German, too — 'Amsel' sounds much better than 'blackbird'."

Merle looked up from the menu. "You seem to be good at languages," she remarked.

The waiter took their order, and Walton's new friend resumed the conversation. "I'm glad you like my name. Do you know of any other interesting names?"

"Well... there's Dorothy, which means 'gift from God'... and Benjamin, meaning 'son of my right hand'... and Philip means 'lover of horses'. Which school do you go to? I'm sure it can't be ours — I would certainly have seen you!"

"Stewartson's," she replied with a smile. "I believe you're in Year 10 like me?"

Her schoolboy escort confirmed this to be true. "I'm glad we're the same age," he commented. "I'll be 15 at the end of this month."

Merle's birthday was in August. As they enjoyed their pizzas she learned that Walton had two brothers and one sister. She herself would have liked a sister, but had just one brother.

"Shall we go to Epping Forest for a walk in the woods when we've finished lunch?" the teenage celebrity suggested. "We could go by bus."

Merle approved of the idea, so Walton looked for times of buses on his smartphone. As he did so he grew irritated by news items continually appearing and obscuring what he was trying to look at. Some of them proclaimed: 'Muslim cleric denounces Wonder Boy's comment about Prophet Muhammad', and 'Muslim leaders castigate Wonder Boy for insulting the Prophet'.

"I didn't insult him," Walton protested.

"Didn't insult who?"

"Mohammed, the Muslims' Prophet. In my interview with Adrian Carter I said I thought Mohammed had been misled. I don't consider that insulting."

Merle's deep blue eyes looked thoughtful. "It probably seems *very* insulting to Muslims," she said. However, she decided to change the subject. "Did you find any suitable bus times?" she enquired.

"There's one at 2.15 and one at 2.45. Shall we have a coffee or a cold drink, and then go along to the bus station?"

"OK, an apple juice for me, please."

⸺◈⸺

The weather stayed fine and warm throughout the afternoon, so the two new friends enjoyed their exploration of that part of the forest and also the opportunity to get to know each other.

They found some of the trees particularly interesting. "Look at that one!" Merle exclaimed. It had angular branches; some of them looking almost exactly to be right angles. "How do you think it developed branches like that?" she wondered.

Walton studied the tree thoughtfully. "It's mysterious, isn't it... I can only guess that there were once a lot of other trees growing very close to it, so that the branches had to grow that way and those other trees presumably got cut down over time."

"Maybe," replied Merle, "I s'pose it was something like that."

41

They stopped for refreshments at a wildlife nature centre before going to the bus stop. They were enjoying some delicious ice cream which was described as "locally produced", when Walton's phone tinkled its melody. It was Gareth. He sounded agitated, which was not at all usual for him — he tended to be quiet compared to Ollie and Walton.

"Is that you, Walt? Have you heard the news?"

"What news d'you mean?"

"That Ayatollah in the Middle East has issued a fatwa against you! You're to be put to death, and the person who kills you will be given a big reward!"

"Didn't anyone tell him I'm just a schoolboy saying what I think?" responded Walton, wondering what he should do about it. "Thanks for letting me know, Gareth. I s'pose I'll have to go into hiding. Don't call me again. Hopefully I'll find a way of keeping in touch. Bye."

CHAPTER 7

Where to hide?

Merle stared in horror at her escort. She had clearly heard what Gareth had to say on Walton's phone, and was aghast with anguish. "What are you g'nna do?" she gasped.

Walton rubbed his chin thoughtfully. "I'll have to find somewhere to stay for a while — somewhere people won't connect with me at all..."

"Did you tell your friends you had a date with me?"

"No... come to think of it, I didn't. They were too taken up with talking about Ollie's dad not getting on that plane, and about the blind woman that Jesus healed last Tuesday evening."

"Maybe my parents wouldn't mind you staying with us for a couple of months. We've got a room we call the guest room."

"But they've never met me!"

"No, but they've heard a lot about you, and Mum watched you on the Adrian Carter Show. She seemed quite impressed. Pull your cap well down, and let's go and get the bus."

They got off the bus near Southern Way and walked to Merle's house in Latton Brook. Her mother, who was a French teacher at a different school, had been writing reports.

Mrs O'Brien seemed genuinely pleased to meet Walton. She invited them into the kitchen where there was a breakfast bar with stools. Seated on these with a cup of tea, the two new friends explained Walton's predicament.

"Oh no!" she expostulated. "How could the Ayatollah do that, considering you're just a 14-year-old schoolboy! I suppose it was because you said it on television, for all the world to hear. Well, if you're looking for a hiding place, I'd be happy for you to stay here, and I expect Alan, my husband, wouldn't mind either. He's been in Scotland for a few days on business, but should be back this evening."

"Oh, that would be great! I don't think *anyone* has any idea where I am! But it's wonderful of you to offer me accommodation when you don't even know me!"

"Well, I've seen you on TV several times, and what's really wonderful is what has been happening on Tuesday nights at Kingsmount Church! A woman with MS healed, and a blind woman getting her sight back!"

"Well, I suppose you realise it isn't actually me who works these miracles. I just pray, and Jesus does the rest!"

As they were talking, Merle's brother Liam appeared from upstairs. He was nearly as tall as the boy he was now introduced to, and Walton learned that he was 3 years older than his sister. He looked excited by the news, including the invitation to the boy to stay indefinitely in the 'guest room'.

"If it's too risky for you to phone your parents, I don't mind taking messages, if you tell me where you live."

"Well," said his mother, "if you don't mind doing that, maybe you could bring back Walton's toothbrush and other things that he might need."

It was decided that Mrs O'Brien would drive Liam to Primrose Park, but would drop him a few roads away, in case the house was already being watched.

With the curtains closed Walton and Merle now felt able to relax as they sat chatting side by side on the sofa. "Well, life is certainly full of surprises these days," Walton remarked. "But I was looking forward to seeing my grandma, who was coming to stay with us till Monday. We don't see her very often; she lives in Wainbridge, near Weston-super-Mare."

"Oh, how disappointing for you. My grandparents live in Chelmsford, so we see them quite often. At least, that applies to Mum's parents. My Dad's parents are in Ireland, but they come over quite a lot. We call them Nan and Pops. They enjoy sightseeing while they're here, or visits to the theatre in London."

"I've switched off my phone," Walton announced somewhat sadly. "It's a precaution; but it feels weird not to be able to text or talk to any of my friends and family."

Merle thought she heard a car come to a stop on the drive in front of the house. "Are they back already?" she wondered. But no; it was her father returning from his business trip to Scotland.

Mr O'Brien settled himself in an armchair to listen to the youngsters' account of how the boy came to be in his present situation. "I've got no objection to having you staying with us for a while," he assured the boy, realising that the unexpected guest was hoping for such confirmation of what his wife had assumed. "I'm sure we can keep you well hidden for as long as necessary," he added with a smile which seemed to light up his face.

A car could be heard pulling up on the road outside. Merle sprang up and ran to open the front door. She was surprised to see four people emerge from her mother's car. Who had they brought with them? Mrs O'Brien escorted a woman with black, slightly greying bushy hair into the house, and a girl

— the new boyfriend's sister Esther. Walton was delighted to see his much-loved Grandma.

"It's great to see you, Grandma!" he exclaimed after she released him from her usual bear-hug. "I thought I was going to miss you, thanks to a certain ayatollah. Did you bring Smudger with you?"

"Yes. Esther took him for a walk earlier on, so he didn't mind being made comfortable in his basket in the garage."

Walton was very fond of Smudger, a black spaniel with long silky hair that Grandma had had since he was a puppy about 6 years ago.

"Well, you've found some good friends here," said his grandma warmly, with a bright smile directed around at the O'Brien family. "God will protect you, and it looks as if Mr and Mrs O'Brien will really help you."

"We certainly will!" Merle's father agreed. "What have you got there, Lynn?" he added, noticing that his wife was carrying a large plastic bag into the kitchen.

"We picked up chicken and chips on the way back," she announced.

Esther had come along so that she could escort Grandma back to the house in Primrose Park after being dropped off some distance away.

Thus they believed they were succeeding so far in keeping Walton's' whereabouts a secret.

CHAPTER 8

A safe house?

As Merle was walking to school on Monday morning she was feeling glad that she had not mentioned her date with Walton to any of her friends. She had decided to wait till after the event before talking about it, in case the Wonder Boy didn't consider her worth spending his time on. When her best friend, Lizzie, had texted her yesterday, she had told her friend that she needed to get her homework done. This was true although she usually tried to avoid doing homework on Sundays; this time she didn't have much choice for various reasons.

Lizzie and two other friends, Gemma and Cheryl, got together with Merle in their classroom before registration. All the groups of friends throughout the room were buzzing with excitement about the Wonder Boy and the death threat hanging over him. "I hope they don't find him!" said Lizzie, the expression on her face of fearful apprehension tending to belie her words.

"It'll be difficult for him to stay hidden, won't it?" suggested Gemma, a small girl who wore stylish glasses and her brown hair in a pony tail.

They all agreed that it would be very difficult. "But I don't think our police will help the Muslims look for him," said Merle. "I think Salman Rushdie was given advice by the police about how to stay in hiding. He didn't get caught, did he?"

Some of her friends thought not, but were not sure. "The trouble is, most people have seen pictures of Walton Dorsey in the papers or seen him on television," said Gemma in tones of concern. "It'll be really difficult for him to go anywhere without being recognised."

Merle had been right about the role of the police. The previous day a police officer had visited Walton's family to offer any help or advice his parents might need. He seemed pleased that they apparently did not know their son's whereabouts. As he was leaving, he assured them that his colleagues were willing to help in any way if needed. "We like to prevent murder from happening, as well as bringing murderers to justice," he declared.

At Passwords School there was even more excitement than at Stewartson's. The whole school seemed to be standing around outside the main entrance, vociferously discussing the Wonder Boy's menacing situation.

"I can't believe you don't know where he is!" said Malcolm Black somewhat belligerently to Ollie, Gareth and a few other friends.

"Well, it's true, whether you believe it or not," retorted Ollie. "He seems to have switched off his mobile, and his mum says she doesn't know where he is at the moment."

"I wish we could do something to help him," said Gareth plaintively.

"You know what Walton would say — 'just pray'!" responded Ollie, "it's the least we can do."

"No," came a strong, deep voice from behind, "it's not the least, it's the **best** you can do!" It was their RE teacher, endeavouring to negotiate his way to the main entrance.

"OK Mr Farley," said Ollie, "we'll expect you to join us in doing just that!"

Mr and Mrs Dorsey had been greatly relieved to learn from Grandma that their middle son was being looked after by a really nice family. They had also appreciated Merle's brother Liam's offer to act as a go-between for his sister's new boyfriend.

The ravenous paparazzi and other media vultures who had rapidly gathered Saturday afternoon outside their home not long after news of the fatwa broke, had gradually dwindled after Mrs Dorsey stood outside the front door and made a statement:

"I can assure you that we have absolutely no idea where Walton is," she declared loudly and clearly. "He went out this morning without saying where he was going, and we haven't seen him or heard from him since. We are praying for his protection, and trust that God will keep him safe."

Some of the reporters were satisfied with her statement; others insisted on asking questions about how she felt. "It may not surprise you to hear that my husband and I love our son Walton;" she said, "but if you're unable to imagine how it feels to be told that your son's life is in this kind of danger, perhaps you need to consult a psychiatrist who deals with emotional problems!"

Eventually the inquisitors drifted away and left the Dorsey family in peace.

Liam kept his promise on Sunday afternoon and Mrs Dorsey lent him one of her eldest son Nathan's caps in the hope that some of the neighbours might think it was Nathan.

However, Liam had already left when Ollie called at 99 Primrose Park to try to find out where Walton might be hiding. "He seems to have switched off his mobile," he complained to Mr Dorsey while his wife was making a pot of tea.

Before answering Ollie's question, Mr Dorsey said, "Hang on a minute." He went out of the front door and looked around. "I was just checking," he explained as he came back in, "so far there don't seem to be any eavesdroppers anywhere outside listening in to our conversation. Yes, switching off his phone was a wise move on Walton's part, you never know who might be listening to phone calls or reading your emails these days."

While the three of them enjoyed a cup of tea, Mrs Dorsey explained how their son had been invited to stay at the home of his new girlfriend.

"I didn't know he had a girlfriend," said Ollie in surprise.

"Neither did we; but it seems like an ideal solution, so that no one has any idea where he might be."

"What about Esther and Leo; do they know?"

"Esther does, but we thought it would be too much to expect a seven-year-old to keep a secret like that. The Ayatollah isn't joking!" said Mr Dorsey grimly.

"The girlfriend's name is Merle, and she has an older brother called Liam," Mrs Dorsey told him. "He volunteered to bring written messages from Walton to ourselves or to you. But thinking about it, I'm not so sure that would be a good idea. I think somebody might get suspicious if they kept seeing Liam," she continued, "they might follow hm..." She sighed, looking at Ollie rather helplessly.

"Can I do something to help?" he responded. "There must be something we can do..."

They considered the possibilities for a few minutes, then Mrs Dorsey said, "Ollie, would you be willing to meet up with Liam somewhere after school — maybe Tye Staples shopping centre?"

"OK, I wouldn't mind," Ollie replied, "there's a café where they have some really good ice cream — mmm, yummy!"

"The trouble is," said Mrs Dorsey thoughtfully, "we don't know when Liam will be coming here again. It may be tomorrow; it may not. It's really problematic trying to manage without a phone!"

"Oh well, I'll ride my bike over there every day after school till I meet up with him. Tell him to look out for a Passwords blazer. Did you hear Walton's been sighted in Cornwall?"

"No!" responded Mr and Mrs Dorsey simultaneously. "We heard he'd been spotted in Scotland," the former declared with a wry smile.

⊷⊶

Meanwhile, Jeff was feeling gutted by the news of the fatwa. He had acquired a deep respect and admiration for Walton Dorsey, and now it looked as if he would be off the radar for an indefinite time, assuming that he didn't get murdered... Jeff had been looking forward to seeing and hearing the lad on Tuesday evening. 'Maybe he will show up after all,' he thought. 'P'r'aps he'll disguise himself.' He decided to get a Bible tomorrow in the Christian bookshop not far from where he worked in Harrison's, and go to Kingsmount Church straight after work. 'That way I should be early enough to get a seat, and I can read my new Bible while I'm waiting.'

When he arrived there at 5.40 Tuesday evening he was indeed early enough to find a seat; in fact, a seat in the fifth row from the front. He settled down feeling happy and hopeful, with the sandwich he had bought from the store where he worked, and finding some interesting incidents involving Jesus in his Bible. It was a modern version, not like the one his mother had, which was in old English, full of thees and thous and a lot of stuff that he didn't understand. This was different.

At approximately 7 o'clock Pastor Robnott started the proceedings. He apologised on behalf of Walton Dorsey for the boy's absence, but assumed that everyone present had heard about the fatwa threatening his life. "All of us here at Kingsmount Community Church are praying for his protection," he said, "and we hope you will do the same."

After a few songs Pastor Robnott made some challenging remarks about lying and speaking the truth. He pointed out that in the majority of movies that involved mystery and suspense, the solutions to the problems were almost always based on lies. "It's an easy way out," he commented. "Too easy, and all too easy for those watching to be led astray into doing the same kind of thing. I challenge script writers to find a solution to their story's problem without resorting to a lie!

"Truth is woven into the fabric of the Universe!" he continued. "Think about it: will the Universe sustain a lie? The answer has to be 'No'. Although it seems that different physical laws apply when particles are studied on the scale of the nanosphere or smaller, and also apparently when it comes to the macrocosmos; nevertheless these different laws will hold good — there is no place in scientific research for dishonesty. Those who try to mislead people with false results of their research are doomed to failure.

"It's a sad fact that there is an alarming lack of truth and honesty in our society today. This is most obvious when we listen to our politicians. How good it would be if they always spoke the truth!" A ripple of laughter greeted this statement, eliciting the further comment by the pastor: "You see how brainwashed we are to consider the idea as laughable. It isn't laughable — it's tragic. The book of Proverbs in the Bible emphasises the importance of honesty and integrity. If you accommodate lies and dishonesty into your life, you are accommodating destruction into the depths of your being. You need to uproot it; dig it out and become a truthful person. Otherwise you will suffer the consequences of your sin.

"Selwyn Hughes relates how when he was in Madras he was told of a milkman there who had to drive his cow to deliver the milk, and milk the cow in the presence of each housewife. Why did he do it in such a wearisome way? Because he had been caught adding water to the milk! So as a result, because he couldn't be trusted, he had to milk the cow before each person he served."

Later in the evening Pastor Robnott introduced a youngish man to the people present named Matthew Lockwood. He looked to be in his late thirties or early forties, with light brown hair and an attractive beard of the same colour. His blue-grey eyes looked friendly, and Jeff realised that it couldn't be the Wonder Boy in disguise, for he was about 5ft 9ins tall.

"Matthew also has a healing ministry in his church in Doncaster," said the pastor. "so if you have come here this evening hoping to be healed of some kind of trouble, whether physical, emotional, psychological or spiritual, I'm sure Matthew's prayers will help, especially if we all pray for the people seeking healing."

Jeff watched as the people who were prayed for turned to go back to their seats. There didn't seem to be any dramatic miracles of healing taking place, but he realised that the healing of internal problems wouldn't be immediately obvious, nor the healing of skin ailments such as acne or eczema. Then he noticed an elderly woman flexing the fingers of both hands as she returned to her seat, and showing the people sitting nearby how flexible they were. Her face revealed a combination of surprise and delight. He guessed that she had been healed of something like arthritis that had made her fingers stiff and unusable. After a while he saw a man aged about 60 who had been leaning heavily on his stick, pass the stick to Matthew Lockwood and walk around the front of the church, smiling broadly.

'Well,' Jeff thought to himself, 'that may not look like a wonderful miracle, but to that guy it probably feels like one!'

At about 10 o'clock Pastor Robnott announced the end of the healing ministry and the opportunity for those who wished to leave, to go now, while others might want to stay till 11.00 pm. He added, "Don't forget that healing is not always instantaneous. Quite often it happens gradually, over a few days, or sometimes weeks. Just remember to say thank you to Jesus for healing you!"

On his way home on the bus Jeff couldn't help imagining what might happen to the Wonder Boy if any would-be assassins succeeded in finding him. Although he hadn't prayed since he was about ten years old, he closed his eyes and prayed silently: "God, please protect Walton Dorsey and prevent any killers from finding him. Amen."

CHAPTER 9

A horrific vision

At 212 Latton Brook Walton awoke on Sunday morning feeling refreshed after a good night's sleep. The bed he was lying on was softer than his own at home, and although that was comfortable enough, he was enjoying this unusual softness. He said a thank You prayer, then thought to himself: 'It's like being on holiday! I'm g'nna think of it that way all the time I have to stay here, and make the best of it. Mrs O'Brien seems to want me to feel at home; she's really kind... and with Merle around, it won't feel much like "house arrest"!'

Hearing sounds of movement downstairs he looked at his watch and saw that it was 9.15. The bathroom door was open, so after a brief visit there he ran downstairs to find out how best to fit in with this hospitable family.

"Good morning Walton," said Mrs O'Brien cheerily, "did you sleep well?"

"I certainly did, thank you — like a sack o' potatoes!"

"That's good. We've got some button mushrooms in the fridge. Would you like some of them sautéed with a fried egg and baked beans for breakfast?"

"Yes please, that sounds great!"

While these were being cooked, Walton sat on one of the stools and discussed with Mrs O'Brien which members of the family usually wanted a shower or wash at what particular time, so that he could fit in when everyone else had finished in the bathroom.

After a few moments they were joined by Merle, who supplied coffee for their guest and tea for her mother and herself. Seated next to Walton and enjoying the same breakfast, she expressed her appreciation for her mother's cooking. "The mushrooms taste really good, cooked like this, cut in quarters!" she enthused. "A lot of people overcook them, and I really dislike the big mushrooms when they're overcooked."

Her new boyfriend agreed with her, but Mrs O'Brien explained that they didn't very often have a cooked breakfast, "Only when we have special guests!" she declared with a merry smile. Next came the choice of marmalade, honey or raspberry jam on the toast. Walton opted for the honey, whilst Merle decided to have half a piece of toast with marmalade, and the other half with honey.

"Sure you don't want jam on it!" quipped Walton.

They had decided to sit with their backs towards the kitchen window, in case any of the neighbours should want to pop in. It was a detached house with a side entrance, similar to the other houses in the row. The kitchen had a door leading to the living room and another leading to the hallway and stairs near the front door.

"We're keeping the back door locked while you're down here," said Merle, "so that if someone knocks on it, you can slip out and disappear upstairs."

"I s'pose I'll have to spend most of the time upstairs," Walton remarked. "What about your friends — do they usually get together with you in your bedroom?"

"Yes, most of the time. I've got a sofa and a club chair. But I'd better try to avoid them coming here. Maybe I can arrange something with Lizzie or Gemma or Emily this afternoon."

"What about this morning? Are you planning to go to church?"

"Sometimes I go to the Anglican-Methodist Church at Tye Staples, but it can sometimes be too formal. Kingsmount seems to be better, at least on Tuesday evenings!"

After breakfast they decided to have their own kind of house church here. "I guess we could probably sing one song without attracting the neighbours' attention," Walton proposed. "Do you play any kind of instrument?"

"Yes, the piano."

"I play the guitar, but I didn't want to lumber your brother with bringing it. What shall we sing?"

"I like the new version of 'The Lord's My Shepherd'," said Merle, sitting at the piano in the living-room and beginning to play the tune by ear.

Their voices blended harmoniously, eliciting some encouragement from Liam, who had now prised himself out of bed and had descended into the kitchen in search of breakfast. Popping his head around the door, he commented, "That sounded really good! You're undiscovered stars!"

At that moment the doorbell rang. Walton dashed into the kitchen, shutting the door behind him. He stood there, listening, waiting for the visitor to go into the living-room. Then he heard a man's voice, which changed from words to hearty laughter, joined by Merle's melodious laugh. He heard them close the front door, and it was Merle who opened the door into the kitchen.

"It's OK Walton," she said reassuringly, "it's only Dad coming back from his walk to the shops to get his paper!"

"Hallo Walton," said Mr O'Brien, "I don't have the *Observer* delivered on Sunday like the *Guardian* during the week. I like to get a bit of exercise."

"Well, it was a useful bit of practice hearing the doorbell," Walton responded. "Merle and I were just doing a bit of house church."

"Yes, I think we'd better do the rest upstairs," said Merle. "Let's go up to my room."

After some prayers and Bible readings they enjoyed a question and answer session. Each posed an apparently awkward question to the other, with some interesting results.

Walton: "Why did Jonah get swallowed by the big fish (which may or may not have been a whale)?"

Merle: "To save his life."

Walton: "Why was he on the ship?"

Merle: "No! It's my turn to ask a question: Why did Balaam's donkey speak to him?"

Walton: "Because he was on his way to put a curse on the Israelites. My turn: Back to Jonah. Why was he on the ship that nearly got wrecked?"

Merle: "Because he didn't want people to laugh at him."

Walton: "Brilliant! You got it in one! God wanted him to preach to the people of Nineveh to get them to change their ways otherwise disaster would strike. Jonah believed that if they repented, God would prevent the disaster from happening and he would end up looking a fool. Your turn."

Merle: "How do you suppose Joseph and Mary managed to live, apparently without much money, when they escaped into Egypt with their baby Jesus?"

"Well, I've never actually considered that one... What's the answer?"

"Well you know the Magi presented Jesus with gold, among other things; so I think they were probably able to use some of that to pay for what they needed in Egypt until Joseph could establish himself as a carpenter."

"Mmm, OK Merle, that sounds reasonable. You win!"

In the afternoon Merle texted her friend Lizzie, who agreed to meet up at Gemma's house and see what they might want to do.

Walton spent a while surfing the net, appreciating the fact that Merle had put her computer at his disposal. They both realised that it would be all too easy for him to be traced through his Internet contacts, even though he didn't use Facebook or Twitter.

Flashes of news told him that the Wonder Boy had been sighted in Blackpool, and that certain groups of extremists in Egypt had vowed to find this infidel who had insulted the Prophet, and to obey the fatwa.

The days passed extraordinarily slowly for the boy celebrity, even though each member of the O'Brien family had offered him some really interesting books. Ollie had made contact with Liam, so they were able to exchange messages that way. As promised, Ollie had cycled to Tye Staples after school on Monday. He enjoyed one of the local ice creams, sittng at one of the tables outside the café, but didn't get himself a drink. 'I may have to do this every day this week till I meet up with Liam,' he thought, 'I don't want to run out of pocket money.'

However, he didn't have to wait that long. On the following day he was joined at his table by a tall year twelve wearing a Stewartson's blazer.

"Hi, is your name Ollie by any chance?" he asked in his usual friendly tone.

"You guessed right. So you're Liam, right?" said Ollie in a quieter voice than usual. He had become aware of a man with a black beard sitting about four metres away, who had seemed to be staring at him. He said even more quietly, "I'm going into Marston's — meet me in there after a bit." He stood up, saying, "See you later."

Liam got himself an orange juice, which he drank in the café, then strolled along to Marston's Minimarket in search of Walton's faithful friend. He discovered him surveying the array of sweets and chocolate bars.

"Hi, did you see that guy with the beard?" Ollie wondered, "I thought we'd better play it safe." He surreptitiously withdrew a medium-sized envelope out of his pocket and passed it to the older boy, who came closer and was able to slip the envelope into one of his own pockets in a way that they both hoped was unobtrusive.

After their first meeting Ollie had kept the Passwords school badge on his blazer out of sight, to avoid attracting attention by his meetings with the older boy, and they varied the actual meeting point — sometimes in the café, sometimes in the minimarket or one of the other shops.

However, what made Walton's stay at 212 Latton Brook really enjoyable was the opportunity to get to know Merle. Some evenings she needed to finish off some homework or meet up with her friends, but sometimes they were able to watch a movie together in her room or enjoy a game of Scrabble. Sometimes they asked each other questions not directly related to the Bible.

"Why do you think God created the dinosaurs?" Merle asked.

"I've often wondered about that, and now I'm sure the answer is: to fertilise the soil of the world! It seems obvious to me now. Such enormous creatures produced enormous amounts of excrement, which was then spread over most of the continents until they were wiped out by the meteor 65 million years ago. The Earth was then fertile enough, ready to produce all the various plants and creatures that God would create to develop interdependently."

"Wow! That definitely sounds like the answer! Where did you discover that?" Merle responded.

"I've never read it or heard it anywhere. It just occurred to me that that must be the answer."

Merle looked at him admiringly. After thinking about that scenario for several minutes, she said, "Have you got an awkward question for me?"

"Well, the answer to this one has to be just an opinion. Do you think there's intelligent life anywhere else in the Universe?"

Merle smiled with a distant look in her eyes. "It depends entirely on whether or not God wanted any other planets to support intelligent beings. If He did, the answer, of course, is 'Yes'; otherwise it has to be 'No', because so many factors have to be just right for such complex creatures as ourselves to develop. Some people seem to think if we were the only intelligent creatures, all the rest of the Universe would be 'wasted' or 'not worth God taking the trouble to create it'!

"Here's another one for you," she added. "What do you think of the so-called 'Creationists'?"

"I think they should read Dr Denis Alexander's book 'Creation or Evolution: Do We Have to Choose?' He's a Christian microbiologist who does ongoing research into DNA. And as for people who insist on believing that the Earth and everything on it was created in six days..." Walton rolled his eyes upward, "I don't know why they find it so difficult to accept that the word 'day' in chapter 1 of Genesis represents a period of time. Elsewhere in the Bible it says a day is like a thousand years in God's sight. And I believe the Adam and Eve story was meant to be understood as an allegory — like 'Pilgrim's Progress'. I think the people who lived in Abraham's time understood it that way. They were used to imagery. Hebrew and Arabic literature is full of it."

"It seems that sticking literally to everything in the Bible goes back a long way," said Merle. "I've been reading 'Mountains on the Moon' by Michael Arthern, and he describes Galileo's struggle with the church leaders at that time, who refused to believe that there could be mountains on the moon, or that it reflected the sun's light. But Galileo seemed to believe that nothing the scientists discovered could actually contradict the Bible. From our point of view the moon *is* a light, as the Bible says."

On Wednesday evening of the second week the movie finished just before 10 pm, so Walton squeezed the hand of this adorable girl, stood up and said, "It's time to say goodnight," gave her a brief kiss on the cheek, and went along to what was now regarded as "his room".

The following evening Merle had to get an English essay written by next day. Walton spent the evening reading a book lent to him by Liam on quantum physics. It was heavy going, but he forced himself to keep trying to understand it. By 10.30 he had had enough. 'I still can't believe that something can be in two places at once!' he said to himself as he closed the book.

As he was waking up next morning Walton was confronted by a terrifying vision. He saw his grandma's house in Wainbridge, and behind it a gigantic wave was surging up the Bristol Channel, spreading out to submerge everything on both sides of the channel. The wave looked to be about 25 metres high! After a few moments the vision faded, leaving him shaking with terror as he lay there. Was this another warning from God? he wondered. If so, what could he do about it?

CHAPTER 10

"I'm willing to risk it"

Walton lay there, trying to grapple with the mental and emotional shock as he contemplated some of the effects that a tsunami would have all around the Bristol Channel if his 'vision' was a warning from God, as the previous one had been. If so, he would have to let people know about it... especially Grandma! Hus thoughts turned to Liam. He would probably be willing to help.

The day dragged by even more slowly than usual as he waited for Liam to come home from school. However, it was Merle who arrived home, before her brother, and came up to see him carrying a small tray with two cups of tea and several biscuits. Walton waited till she had had a chance to have some refreshment, then described to her the appalling vision he had been presented with.

"A tsunami! In Britain?!!" she gasped, "I thought they only happened in certain areas — like earthquake zones."

Walton shook his head. "No, apparently they can happen in a lot of other places. I remember watching a documentary on TV about one that hit the Bristol Channel in the Middle Ages. I think it was near the beginning of the seventeenth century."

"Ohh-h-h... so it really could happen..." Merle responded in anguish.

Liam agreed to take a message to Walton's mother, asking her to phone her mother in Wainbridge to warn her about the vision and the probable tsunami.

Mr O'Brien arrived home just after 5 o'clock, thanks to the flexitime operated by his company whereby employees were able to accumulate work-free hours by starting one or two hours earlier on certain days. His reaction to the news of Walton's vision was similar to that of the boy himself: an urgent desire to warn as many people as possible.

"We need to let the media know about it — but without using a phone or email," said the teenage celebrity thoughtfully.

Mr O'Brien was equally thoughtful. Then he said: "Well, if you write a note to the news editor of the *Guardian*, I'll take it to their offices in London tomorrow, and hopefully they'll pass it on to the rest of the media."

"Oh, that'd be great! Thanks a million!" said Walton with a thumbs-up sign of approval.

When Liam returned from his visit to Primrose Park, however, his news was not good. Mrs Dorsey had been unable to reach her mother. Her landline carried the message that her voicemail box was full and could therefore accept no new messages, and her mobile phone was switched off.

Now Walton was seriously worried. He couldn't imagine why Grandma wasn't answering her phone. "OK Liam," he said, forcing himself to express his thanks in a sincere way, "thanks very much for going to Primrose Park and trying to warn my grandma about the danger."

"You're welcome," Liam responded in his usual friendly tone. "I'd better get a bit of homework done."

As Liam went out and closed the door behind him Walton reflected that he had not only gained a new girlfriend: her brother had also become a good friend. Then he ran a hand through his hair and considered what to do to help Grandma...

After praying and turning things over in his mind, he knew that there was just one way open to him. He would take the train down to Weston-super-Mare. What about money for the fare? He had about £250 saved up in his Post Office bank account, which he had earned from his paper round, but he couldn't risk accessing that. Maybe Mr O'Brien could lend him some.

He continued pondering over what he would do, until Merle came upstairs carrying a tray bearing a plateful of spaghetti bolognaise.

"That smells wonderful!" he enthused. "I needed cheering up—"

"And I need to put this tray down, if you would be so kind..."

"Oh, sorry!" her penitent boyfriend replied as he jumped up and seized the small fold-away table they used for his meals, and set it up as fast as possible so that his beloved could put the tray down. "Have you heard about my grandma not answering her phone?"

"Yes; I'm not surprised you're concerned about her. I agree with you that she's a lovely person, even though I only had a short time to get to know her. Anyway, I'd better go down and eat my spaghetti before it gets cold. Bon appétit!"

"Same to you. Merle, would you ask your dad to come up for a few minutes when he's finished eating, please?"

"OK. See you later."

Mr O'Brien fully understood Walton's concern about his grandmother. "There's probably a quite reasonable explanation," he said, "but of course we have no clues to tell us what that might be."

"Well I'm going down there to find out what's going on. I'll get a train to Weston-super-Mare, and probably a bus or a taxi to Wainbridge."

Mr O'Brien stared at him, aghast. He had become very fond of this unusual boy in the short time he had been staying in the guest room.

"*No!*" he expostulated, "You can't do that! Someone would be sure to trace your movements!"

"Maybe, maybe not. Anyway, I'm willing to risk it. I'm going — if you can lend me £150, please. I'll pay you back; I've got £250 saved up in my bank account, but I can't get at it, can I."

"Walton, **please** don't do it! You'll be putting yourself in double jeopardy, and I'm not joking. You'll be in danger from would-be assassins and also from the tsunami if there is one. You probably wouldn't be able to help your grandma, anyway. **Please** think it over."

"I *have* thought it over. And while I'm on the train I'm planning to email all the churches around the Bristol Channel. What advice would you give to the people who think their church building is important? Is there any way they could protect it?"

Mr O'Brien considered the question for a few moments, then he replied tentatively, "Well… there's not much that can be done, but the building could be given a certain amount of protection by piling up sandbags around it in a kind of molehill shape. But I don't suppose there'd be many people volunteering to do something like that if their own house were in danger of being demolished!"

"Thanks for the advice, anyway. I'll email your suggestion to the churches. There may be some people who really care a lot about their church building, and would be glad of the chance to help. But I'm still hoping you can lend me £150. Can you?"

"Oh, alright," Mr O'Brien replied, shrugging his shoulders with resignation. "It's obviously no use trying to get you to change your mind. I'll go along to Tye Staples and get the money." He picked up the tray with the plate and cutlery and disappeared out of the room while the grateful teenager endeavoured to express his thanks.

CHAPTER 11

Getting a warning into the public domain

It wasn't long after her dad descended the stairs before Merle was knocking on Walton's door. "Dad says you're planning to go to Weston-super-Mare!" she exclaimed incredulously. "*By train!* You can't be serious, surely!"

"Oh yes; I'm definitely serious!" Walton assured her. "I want to find out why Grandma isn't answering her phone, and try to make sure she doesn't get swept away!"

"But Dad said you're planning to use your tablet on the train! Some people are sure to trace you!"

"Maybe — maybe not. I don't think it'll be that easy for anyone to do so. Anyway, as I told your dad, I'm willing to risk it. Shall we watch a movie?"

"How can you think of watching a film when you're about to put your life in real danger — either from the murderers or from the tsunami?!"

"Well, if it's a good film it'll take our minds off any danger for a while." He took her hand and pulled her firmly but gently towards her room. "What's on offer for this evening?"

Some of the films they considered involved marriages breaking up as one partner falls in love with someone else. Merle preferred not to watch that kind of storyline. "I don't like films about adulterous relationships," she said. "I believe we were created to be monogamous."

"Yes, I'm sure that was God's intention," Walton agreed. "Unfortunately it seems that such couples are in the minority these days."

"I'm sure it's mainly the result of promiscuity among teenagers. If they get married, they don't have the unique physical bond they were meant to have. I intend to keep my virginity till I'm married."

The look that Walton gave her held a blend of warm love and admiration, as he lifted her hand to his lips.

They decided to watch a film with a quite complicated plot involving a couple getting to know each other through a web of mysterious emails, which the two teenagers watched as they sat side by side on Merle's sofa. It was soon holding their attention as the plot thickened, only to be interrupted by a somewhat unwelcome knock at the door. It was Mr O'Brien. "I'm sorry Walton," he said, "the cash machine at Tye Staples had run out of cash. I didn't use the car, as I thought the exercise would do me good. Can we leave it till the morning? I can try our bank in the town centre. I think it's open for a couple of hours on a Saturday morning. I've got some work I need to finish this evening."

"OK," the boy celebrity replied in a pleasant tone, "I don't suppose it'll make any difference. Thanks for tryng."

Merle enjoyed the movie; it did indeed help to distract her from negative thoughts. Walton, however, found himself continually considering possible scenarios involving Grandma or what he himself should do. As the film came to an end he stood up, saying, "Time to say goodnight."

Merle got up off the sofa likewise, commenting, "I enjoyed that; I thought it was really good."

Walton put his arms around her, looking into her large deep-blue eyes. "We won't be seeing each other for a while. I'm really g'nna miss you. You know what rhymes with 'miss'?" He folded her more snugly in his arms and gave her a long, slow, tender and romantic kiss on the lips. Then he strode to the door, gave her a wave of his hand and a smile, and went along to "his" room.

Merle stood there for a few moments as if rooted to the spot; then she sank dreamily onto the sofa, savouring the experience of that kiss, when it had seemed as if she had been floating on air with Walton in a magical dream.

Next morning Mr O'Brien came up to Walton's room immediately after breakfast. At his suggestion his young guest wrote a note by hand to the news editor of the *Guardian*, including a request that he pass on the news to other media. They arranged that Walton would go to the train station with Mr O'Brien in his car, lying down on the rear seats under a travelling rug including while the latter obtained the desired cash from the bank. It was uncomfortable trying to keep in basically the same position even for ten minutes, but the minutes dragged on into half an hour before Mr O'Brien at last returned to the car park with the cash.

He opened the door nearest to the teenager's head, bent down as if packing something away, and said quietly, "The bank doesn't open till 10 o'clock, and there was quite a queue at the cash machine." He stuffed the money that Walton had requested under the rug near the boy's hand and took his seat behind the steering wheel, leaving the young celebrity to get hold of the banknotes and stow them in his pocket.

Halfway down the hill leading to the station Mr O'Brien pulled over to the kerbside to let his passenger get out. Walton retrieved his travel bag, slammed the door and began walking down the hill. Merle's helpful dad had lent him one of his old shirts and an old jacket which they thought made him look considerably different from the photographs and TV clips in the media. He was also wearing the baseball cap and sunglasses, so he was hopeful that no one would recognise him.

The middle-aged man who supplied him with a ticket to Liverpool Street didn't seem to pay much attention to his appearance, so he felt reasonably relaxed as he strolled onto the appropriate platform. He discovered that he had missed the train boarded by Merle's dad, so he looked for someone to give him information about the next train. There didn't seem to be anyone about who could tell him, but eventually he found a youngish member of the station staff who said, "The 11.15 to Liverpool Street's been cancelled. The next one after that's the 12.35, but that's only goin' as far as Cheshunt. There'll be a bus from there to Liverpool Street. They're workin' on the line."

Having delivered this vital piece of information with hardly a pause for breath, he walked away rapidly before the tall schoolboy had a chance to thank him for his help. Walton looked at his watch. 10.05. He groaned inwardly: 2½ hours to wait! He took a deep breath and decided to accept the situation. A cup of coffee would be good for starters. The Coffee Shop offered some appetising-looking muffins, including some with blueberries — his favourite.

There were only a few people sitting at the tables, so he made himself comfortable about 3 or 4 metres from the other passengers. The coffee was surprisingly good, and he enjoyed two blueberry muffins. Then he began serious consideration of how he might spend the rest of the time. Could he use his tablet to alert churches? No, he would be traceable here in Harlow. He would have to wait till he was on the train before using it. He had brought his mobile phone with him in case he wanted to use it; but no, that would probably be easier to trace. However, there was another option: pray.

Meanwhile Mr O'Brien's train had reached Liverpool Street. He took the underground to the appropriate station, but before leaving the station he went into the men's toilet and put on a somewhat shabby old raincoat and a floppy trilby-style hat which he had brought with him in a plastic carrier bag. At the *Guardian* offices he pulled the hat down as far as possible and handed the envelope containing Walton's note, addressed to the news editor, to the receptionist. He turned quickly and keeping his head bent downwards left the building, looking for a suitable place to remove his "disguise". However, just at that moment he noticed a taxi approaching, and to his relief it stopped to allow him to make use of it. He gave his destination as the Bank underground station, knowing that it had multiple entrances and levels. Here he was able to find a toilet where he removed the unwanted articles of clothing, restoring them to the plastic shopping bag. He decided to walk above ground to Liverpool Street station.

As soon as the *Guardian* news editor read Walton's note, he transmitted it to the main national news agency without delay, remembering the Wonder Boy's previous vision and how James Patel considered that the schoolboy had thereby saved his life. The news was then passed to the editor of the *Observer* for inclusion in next day's paper. He, in turn, contacted the best-known British seismologists, asking them to let the *Observer* or the *Guardian* know immediately if there was any unusual activity on the seabed around Iceland or in the vicinity of Ireland. He then telephoned his brother, who lived in Swansea.

By the time the 12.35 train arrived at Harlow station Walton had consumed two Cornish pasties, a cherry muffin, another with blueberries and a Mars bar, plus orange juice and more coffee.

He was glad to see that there were not a great many passengers boarding the train, and was able to find a seat far enough away from any inquisitive fellow-travellers. On his tablet he located churches in Bristol, Weston-super-Mare, Ilfracombe, Newport, Cardiff and Swansea, with the message: "If you think your church building is worth trying to protect from the likely tsunami, get as many sandbags as possible as soon as possible, and if time permits, get your worshippers to spend tomorrow piling up the sandbags around the building like a molehill. Please forward this to other local more rural churches. Blessings. Walton Dorsey." Having clicked on Send, he felt a bit happier. Then it occurred to him that the Muslims would probably feel gutted if their mosques were demolished, so he repeated the procedure, finding the addresses of the mosques in those towns. He wondered about synagogues. The only ones he could find were in Bristol and Cardiff; these he alerted likewise.

He was further relieved to see news flashes, such as "Wonder Boy warns of tsunami soon to hit Bristol Channel". But what about Grandma? He decided to use his mobile, and dialled her landline number. But the only response was a recorded voice informing him that no more messages were being accepted. His attempt to reach her on her mobile was equally in vain; it was switched off.

CHAPTER 12

'Am I being followed?'

The promised bus was waiting outside Cheshunt station when Walton's train arrived there, and it reached Liverpool Street Station at 13.10. By this time he was ready for some more refreshment, so he bought himself an apple juice, after which he headed for the Underground. He arrived at Paddington Station at about quarter to two, and consulted the departures indicator. It seemed to be full of the word "CANCELLED". This included trains to Exeter and Penzance, which would normally stop at Weston-super-Mare. He spoke to a middle-aged man who was also staring at the information board. "Excuse me, do you know why so many trains are cancelled?" he asked politely.

"They keep doin' this," the man growled angrily. "They tell us they can't get the drivers. If they paid 'em enough there'd be plenty o' drivers!"

"Yes, you're probably right," agreed Walton, who was now wondering what to do. Then he saw that there was a train to Bristol scheduled for 19.15. At least that would bring him a lot closer to where he wanted to go. 'I'll wait for that one,' he said to himself. He decided to walk around outside the station in the meantime, after a few more snacks.

It was not a particularly pleasant area. There were boarded-up premises which seemed to have been shops; there were estate agents, betting shops and one or two second-hand bookshops. He spent about 15 minutes in one of these, but wasn't able to concentrate on any of the books because of the need to keep an eye on his travel bag; he didn't want that to get nicked. In one of the other side streets there was a shop displaying various female accessories, including handbags, gloves and scarves. There was one in the form of a headsquare with a multicoloured design. Walton felt sure Grandma would like that one. He was nevertheless pleased to discover that it was not too expensive. As the sales assistant was wrapping up the scarf, she remarked, "I hope that Wonder Boy's got it wrong this time, don't you? It'll be really terrible if it's true!"

"Yes, I agree," said the boy celebrity with a worried look. "I hope people will get away in time if it happens." He screwed up his face as he took the proffered bag containing the headscarf, saying, "Thanks, bye," and ambled out of the shop. 'I'm pretty sure she didn't recognise me,' he thought.

The train arrived at Temple Meads station, Bristol, at 8.30 pm. Grandma was still not answering her phone, so he walked on somewhat aimlessly through the streets, where a considerable number of people were still apparently doing some shopping. He was wondering if there was anywhere that he could spend the night. He hadn't seen any news flashes about unusual activity on the seabed anywhere west of the Bristol Channel... He looked behind him occasionally, wondering, 'Am I being followed?' But he couldn't see anyone behaving furtively.

He had walked about two miles, and noticed that he was now passing an Anglican church where there was something unusual happening. He saw that sandbags were being unloaded from a lorry and left in piles in the churchyard. A man wearing a clerical collar had just finished speaking to the men who were transferring the sandbags from where they were being offloaded by the hoist to an area near the church building. Walton wondered whether the vicarage was close by, so he followed, catching up with the probable vicar as he walked down a path that did indeed lead to the vicarage.

The Wonder Boy decided to reveal his identity, assuming that a Christian would certainly not want to help the would-be assassins.

"Good evening, are you the vicar of this church?" he asked hopefully.

"Yes, I am. I'm Martin Johnson, vicar of the Parish of St John's."

"My name is Walton Dorsey — you've probably heard of me—"

"Wonder Boy!" the vicar exclaimed, probably not loudly enough for the men with the sandbags to hear. "Come on in and meet my wife!" He unlocked the front door and ushered the schoolboy celebrity into the hallway. "This way," Rev Johnson added, showing him into the large, comfortable living room. Walton pulled off his cap as he entered, revealing his bushy black hair, and eliciting a squeak of excitement which was quickly modified into: "Oh! It's the Wonder Boy!"

"Yes, I can see that it is now," said her husband, whose darkish brown hair was thinning on top. "I wasn't sure whether to believe him outside." He came closer and shook the boy's hand warmly. "I'm very glad to meet you!" he declared with enthusiasm.

"I'm pleased to meet you, too," replied Walton, "and your wife." He smiled as he shook her hand also. She and her husband looked to be in their late forties or early fifties.

"Do sit down and make yourself at home," Mrs Johnson said in a warm tone, pushing back her light brown hair. "Would you like a cup of tea or coffee?"

"Thank you very much. I really would appreciate a cup o' coffee." He sank gratefully into a comfortable armchair, relaxing against its soft upholst-ery. He had noticed the net curtains covering the windows so that he didn't need to worry about anyone else recognising him.

"So, where have you been hiding?" asked Rev Johnson as the doorbell chimed. He excused himself and went to receive an invoice for the sandbags from one of the men.

Once he had settled down again in another armchair and his wife had passed around coffee and tea together with delicious-looking pieces of cake, the two hosts listened with fascination to the way the Wonder Boy had been provided with an ideal safe house to evade any possible murderers.

"You certainly were very fortunate to have got to know the new girlfriend just at that point in time," commented Rev Johnson.

"It must have been Divine providence," said his wife sagely.

"Well, Mrs Johnson, I thought it was wonderful that her parents let me stay with them, even though they didn't know me!" declared Walton.

"Yes indeed!" the vicar agreed, "but do call us by our first names: Martin and Maxine. And what brings you to this neck o' the woods?"

"I've been trying to contact my grandma for the last couple of days, She hasn't been answering her phone. Her landline mailbox is full, and her mobile has been switched off every time I tried. She lives in Wainbridge."

"Oh dear, I suppose you can't think of anywhere else she might be?" said Maxine.

"No. So I decided to go and see if I can find out what's going on. I thought I would get there today, but a lot of the trains were cancelled." He looked at his watch: 9.55. "Do you usually watch the 10 o'clock news?" he asked. "I'd like to know whether they've found any signs of an earthquake on the seabed."

"Well, we don't always watch it, but we certainly need to know if anything's happening out there," said Martin, getting up and switching on the TV. With the volume turned down to silent, they still had a few minutes to chat. The vicar told Walton that he and his wife and the church secretary had contacted as many of their parishioners as possible, asking those who were able-bodied to come to the church first thing in the morning to build up the sandbags around the church if they considered it worth protecting. There would be a short service at 10 o'clock for those not strong enough to do the sandbagging. And there would be two coaches outside the church on standby to leave for the Taunton area within 10 minutes of any news about a tsunami.

The news, however, was mainly about political events and sport, with some reports of arrangements being made on the South Wales coastline along the shore and in places such as Ilfracombe and Weston-super-Mare in case the seismologists found any signs of earth tremors under the sea.

Rev Johnson turned the sound down and said, "So, no sign of anything yet." He looked at his wife; "Well Maxine, can we offer Walton accommodation for the night? If he feels like it he can help with the sandbagging tomorrow and have a bit of lunch with us?" He was now looking at the boy celebrity, but his wife hastened to agree, "Oh yes, Walton, you're very welcome to stay here for the night. I'll go and get your bed ready." She got up and was halfway out of the room before the teenager could express his thanks.

Walton felt extremely grateful to be able to stretch out and relax in the comfortable bed, and he slept soundly until he was woken by a noise at the window. By the light of the full moon he could see that someone or something was trying to get in through the window from the balcony outside.

CHAPTER 13

A nocturnal disturbance

Walton switched on the bedside lamp and was shocked to see a man climbing into his room. The intruder, who was wearing a black cloth masking his face, muttered something inaudible and pulled a dagger out of his pocket as he advanced towards the boy.

Walton scrambled out of bed, grabbed a pillow and dashed in a nanosecond to the door, shouting as loudly as he could as he opened it, "Help! Help!" Then he turned to face the interloper, holding the pillow as a shield, saying, "You're on the wrong path, my friend…". His would-be murderer faltered, and was frustrated at every thrust of the dagger by Walton's skilful use of the pillow until a few moments later the attacker was confronted by Martin, who was no weakling. He grabbed the assailant's left arm as he attempted to seize the pillow, and twisted it round to his back, while Walton rammed the pillow hard onto the dagger and Martin was able to wrench it out of his grasp.

At that moment Maxine appeared with a coil of rope from what they called the "boots room" next to the back door where they could leave wellies or gardening implements. "The police are on their way," she reported, while Martin and his young friend quickly rendered the intruder helpless as the vicar secured the rope around the fellow's arms and legs while held appropriately by his intended victim.

"Sorry about your pillow," said Walton regretfully as the police dragged the man downstairs, "it has a few lacerations…"

"Not at all, no problem," replied Martin with a smile. "It's a great way to deal with a knife attack!"

"Well, there are no feathers flying about; I suppose it's filled with polyester," Walton remarked, turning it over. "The other side's OK, so I can sleep on that." He put the pillow back in position on the bed, thanked his hosts for their help, climbed back in and wished Martin and Maxine "Goodnight."

He was woken again at 8 a.m. by the alarm on his mobile. There was a washbasin in the room, so after a quick visit to the bathroom he was able to have a wash before going downstairs, where the television was on, with the volume moderately low, but just audible in case the dreaded news came through.

"We don't have much choice for breakfast," said Maxine after they had exchanged good mornings; "Martin likes porridge and I like bran flakes. Would you like either of those, or would you prefer toast and jam or marmalade or honey?"

Walton opted for bran flakes — not as appetising as his favourite cereal, but he thought it helped to show his appreciation for the hospitality provided by Maxine and Martin. However, he was subsequently persuaded to have two slices of toast; first with marmalade, then with honey. "You need to keep up your strength if you're g'nna do the sandbagging," Maxine commented as he munched his toast. "They're unloading two more lorries."

Rev Johnson was already outside helping alongside about 15 early risers of both genders who were hard at work on the west side of the church, placing the sandbags as much like a very thick brick wall as possible while attempting to taper them off as their structure gained height. Walton joined them as soon as he had finished breakfast, again wearing his cap and sunglasses. Gradually the numbers of workers increased, and they spread around each side of the church. A gap of about 10 cm was left between the walls of the church and the "molehill" in the hope that much of the water would be deflected upwards rather than thrusting its weight against the walls. A local man who specialised in producing wooden doors was mounting a kind of wooden framed shutter around the most beautiful of the church's stained glass windows. With two thick pieces of wood fixed diagonally across it, Mr Mills needed the help of two muscular volunteers.

Although Mrs Johnson usually avoided shopping on a Sunday, today she went along to the local convenience store to get three large bottles of milk. However, when after the short worship service she asked the sandbaggers whether they would like tea or coffee, she discovered that the majority had either brought thermos flasks with them or their spouses or partners had come to refresh their other halves with flasks appropriately filled. However, her trip to the shop had not been a waste of time; twelve workers accepted the offer of coffee and five opted for tea. So Maxine, with help from one of the energetic church members, made good use of some of the milk.

By lunchtime it looked as if the efforts of the sandbaggers would probably help considerably to protect the church, including the 16th century stained glass windows. Most of the workers stopped to go home for a bite to eat at about 12.30, and Walton gratefully accepted Maxine's invitation to join the Johnsons for lunch. Maxine had chosen three ready meals out of the freezer. She and Martin usually settled for these on Sundays, so that there was a certain amount of rest for them in spite of Martin's duties involving worship services, christenings and frequent contributions to young people's groups. Throughout the rest of the week Maxine cooked fresh food including green vegetables, with the main course followed by fruit or yogurt, as she knew how important it is to try to avoid chemical additives such as artificial colouring, flavouring and preservatives as far as possible.

While they were eating they were constantly listening for any news. As soon as Martin had finished, he looked at the clock. "Twenty past one," he announced. "Shall we have a coffee before I take Walton to Wainbridge?"

"If he's got his travel bag ready to go, I'll make a quick one," said Maxine, looking enquiringly at their guest.

"I've just got a few things to pack, while you're making it," he replied, heading for the stairs.

As soon as they had drunk their coffee Walton expressed his thanks to Maxine, and boarded Martin's Land Rover Discovery, and they were on their way to Wainbridge. The intrepid schoolboy was glad he had been allowed to recharge the batteries of his mobile and tablet. He had decided that he might need them. He had also considered being surrounded by floodwater, so he had obtained several plastic bags and rubber bands from Maxine, in which he had carefully wrapped his electronic communicators and his Bible.

They left behind the built-up parts of Bristol, ltstening to local radio, but Martin couldn't stand the vocalisations of the music, which he described as "caterwauling", so he turned the volume down low. It wasn't long before they saw signs directing towards the M5, and having driven across this, Portishead came into view in the distance.

"I won't go into the town," said Martin, "I'll skirt round it on the east side." They then got onto the Wainbridge road, which brought them closer to the sea. BUT... where was the water? No water could be seen where it should be!!

"It's the drawback!" shouted Walton. "Stop! Let me get out! We may have 20 minutes or less!" He grabbed his travel bag and jumped out as Martin stopped the car, and Walton shouted, "Get away from the coast!" as he slammed the car door.

CHAPTER 14

Disaster!

After jumping out of Martin's car, Walton stood for a moment looking down at the small town of Wainbridge, then he decided he'd better look for some higher ground. 'I wouldn't be much use trying to help Grandma if I got knocked off my feet and carried away by the waves,' he said to himself. He walked back as fast as he could along the road towards the village they had just driven through, although the ground didn't seem to get much higher. The cars, vans and trucks heading in the same direction grew rapidly into a steady stream, many of them laden almost to overflowing with household articles and bedding. Some of the occupants called out to him, offering a lift, which he at first declined, hoping to be able to go back down to Wainbridge later. But then he changed his mind, accepting a lift offered by an elderly couple on their way to Plymouth. He asked them to drop him off when they reached the village and he saw a pub with the name: 'The Ship and Shovel' evidently including a restaurant, judging by a large sign proclaiming: ALL DAY FOOD. Walton wasn't feeling hungry, but he needed somewhere to wait till the anticipated floodwater subsided sufficiently for him to go down into the little town.

There were still some people sitting at the tables in the restaurant, but Walton headed for the bar, where he ordered an orange juice. "D'you know how far you are here from the sea?" he asked as the bartender filled his glass.

"Yeah, about 10 miles. The big wave probably won't reach us here — except maybe a small amount of flooding."

As he spoke, the water gushed in through the door and filled the place with about a foot of water. Walton grabbed his travel bag off the floor as soon as he felt the water around his feet, placed it on a stool and sat himself on another, pulling his legs up as high as he could.

⋯⋯◉⋯⋯

Grandma, aka Mrs Loretta Green, had in the meantime spent the last two and a half weeks looking after a family in Weston-super-Mare. Her friend Mrs Peggy Wilkinson had a kind of arthritis which was not at all age-related; she had suffered from it since her teenage years, and she was now in her forties. Her husband Paul worked as Chaplain of a local Youth Custody Centre, which entailed frequent periods of intense counselling as well as leading regular activities with the boys. Peggy had needed to go into hospital to undergo tests lasting three weeks, so they had been thankful when Loretta had offered to look after Paul and their three daughters: Hannah aged 15, Martha who was 13 and Sarah aged 9.

Grandma had offered her help in spite of the fact that she worked as a reading assistant in a primary school in Wainbridge. However, as she was there only three days a week for just two lessons each, she assumed that she would be able to cope, and her assumption had been justified.

She had enjoyed the experience. The two older girls were usually helpful and cooperative, in spite of the sounds of a great many episodes of quarrelling emanating from their shared bedroom. Sarah, however, was not so easy to cope with. She enjoyed climbing trees, playing football and darts, and was unwilling to help in any way — even with an undemanding chore such as laying the table or clearing away after a meal. A particular challenge for Loretta's patience had been Sarah's habit of adding tomato ketchup to **every** meal, even to the turkey stew that Loretta considered completely ruined by it. Their father, Paul, was a fun person to have around, continually finding something amusing to say about almost anything. He was not there very often, however, and he had just one irritating habit: if he had a free evening he would sit for what seemed an age flicking through the various channels on the TV while Loretta hoped there might be something worth watching.

But now she had returned to her home in Wainbridge, as Paul had heard the news that there was some ominous activity on the seabed south-west of Ireland. He advised her to get back to her house as fast as possible, collect anything valuable and head to the south, to her son's home near Exeter. Smudger was obviously very pleased to be back home, scampering around with joyful barks.

A helicopter buzzed overhead as she located her passport and birth certificate, which she put in her handbag. She was just adding the handbag to the things already in her travel bag when she heard a different noise — a strange, sinister roaring. Could it be the tsunami?!! She grabbed the travel bag and hurried up the stairs, calling Smudger to come up behind her. Her bedroom window provided a view of the sea at an angle, and as she looked out there was no denying it — a gigantic wall of water was indeed advancing rapidly towards her house!! Sending up a prayer, she clutched Smudger and crawled under the bed as the monstrous wave crashed into parts of the house. She lay there for perhaps ten minutes, shuddering at the second wave and the ominously loud cracking and rumbling in various rooms or ceilings.

Nevertheless she wanted to see, if possible, how deep the water was downstairs. So she crawled out from under the bed. The window was still intact, and she looked out upon the scene of semi-submerged houses and other buildings, whilst single story dwellings were completely covered by the floodwater; otherwise there was not much to be seen but floating debris and destruction. She couldn't tell how deep the water was, but there was no sign of her car which had been on the drive in front of the integral garage.

She started to open her bedroom door, but with a great effort managed to close it again, for she had seen that water was gushing out of the guest room and down the stairs. She grabbed her travel bag, put it on the bed, then she picked up Smudger followed by a tartan blanket which she kept on the top of the chest of drawers, slipped out of her now wet sandals, and, lying on the bed, she wrapped the wet dog in the blanket before reaching down for her sandals. These she dried off on a corner of the blanket. Having placed them on her bedside table, she snuggled up next to Smudger and lay there, trying to reconcile herself to the idea that she would have to wait — either for the water to subside or for someone to rescue her... or both!

─━◉━─

"Are you sure this is a small amount?!!" Walton challenged with a wry smile as the water flooded the 'Ship and Shovel' pub-restaurant.

"Well, I s'pose it could be worse," replied the barman as he waded through the water to fetch a suitable bucket and more water gushed in.

After the second gush came flooding in and it appeared to be settling at that level, all the staff, including the manager, were soon hard at work trying to bale out the water, while the guests in the restaurant were escorted upstairs and given refuge in the owner-manager's lounge. The staff declined Walton's offer of help, saying there were no more buckets. The manager did a great job with a plastic dustbin which he had emptied onto a patch of grass on an area of higher ground in the landscaped garden. He stationed himself near the main door and directed the water from the building towards the road. It didn't prove to be as difficult as they had feared, as the water tended to drain naturally down to the sea. So at last, after several hours, they succeeded in clearing it out of the pub. When they had finally finished the mopping up, the staff were able to sit down in the bar area for a rest. The manager helped to supply tea or coffee all round, including a lemonade for Walton, asking the boy as he did so, "And which way are you heading?"

"I want to find out what's happened to my grandma in Wainbridge," he replied. "She hasn't been answering her phone."

"Oh, no!" he exclaimed with a look of real concern. "When I've drunk my tea we'll have a look and see how much the water's subsiding." He drained his cup, strode to the doorway, and went outside. Walton followed him out. The water had subsided leaving the road clear of water now as far as they could see.

The manager-owner of the pub turned to the boy saying, "My name is Simon Hasenfratz. Let me run you down there in my car, at least as far as possible. I've got a canoe — you could borrow that."

Walton felt choked with gratitude at this; he considered it a wonderful offer and struggled to express his thanks.

"OK, get your bag while I tell my wife what we're doing. I'll bring the car round."

The canoe was already mounted on the roof of the Range Rover. Walton had tried navigating a canoe before, while on holiday, so it didn't take him long to get paddling it towards Grandma's house, through water that he guessed might be about 1½ metres deep, although it was difficult to judge how deep it actually was. He took care to avoid the debris that he could see below the surface. As he came closer to the houses and other buildings he needed to manoeuvre carefully around sunken cars, caravans and other debris such as blocks of masonry. There didn't seem to be anyone else about; hopefully everybody had got away in time, he thought.

When Grandma's house came into view, he was shocked by its horrendous state. Her car had been smashed through the garage door; the front door and surrounding parts and the lower front window had been smashed in, and part of the roof above the garage had collapsed. He was trying to fend off negative thoughts when he heard a dog barking. Smudger?! He stifled a desire to call out the dog's name, for fear Smudger might get himself into a more dangerous place than he was already.

Walton brought the canoe closer to the battered area where the front door had been, and cautiously navigated his way through floating items, such as plastic bowls, wooden objects and pieces of paper, to the stairs. Mr Hasenfratz usually left a length of rope attached to the prow, to be available for remounting the canoe on the car, so Walton was able to use this to tie the canoe to one of the wooden spindles of the banister. He was, of course, on the wrong side of the banister. But this structure proved to be sturdy enough for him to grasp two of the spindles, get his feet onto the edge of the banister and pull himself up. His legs were long enough to enable him to swing them over onto the staircase, and he dashed up to the top.

"Hi, Grandma!" he shouted hopefully.

"Oh-h-h... I'm he-ere," came a thin, strained reply from the room which he recognised as being the guest room.

"Coming, Grandma," he called, stepping carefully between bits of fallen masonry and roof tiles. Then he saw her: lying partly on wet rubble, with a joist from the roof trapping her leg. Smudger was also trapped under part of the bed behind her, while the rest of the bed had collapsed under debris from the roof, which had a jagged hole revealing blue sky and small white clouds beyond the rafters.

"Hi, Grandma," he said again. "Is it very painful?"

"Yes... it is."

"I'll see if I can lift that beam off," he said. But it was far heavier than he'd expected; he couldn't move it. "Phew!" he gasped, "I wonder what kind of wood this is!" He stood up straight and took a deep breath, and prayed that he would be able to lift the wet joist. He took some more deep breaths, went into a squatting position, then lifted the joist off Grandma's leg and onto the floor!

"Praise the Lord!" he shouted.

Grandma's smile was not up to her usual standard, but she managed one nevertheless. "Amen!" she said with an effort.

"D'you think your leg's broken?"

"Yes, I guess it must be," she said. "Is it bleeding much?"

She was not wearing tights or stockings, as she considered the weather was warm enough without them, so Walton had no difficulty checking. "No, amazingly enough, there's just a small amount of blood just above the knee — otherwise things would have been really serious, wouldn't they."

"How did you get here? You don't look very wet."

"Mr Hasenfratz, the manager of the Ship and Shovel pub lent me his canoe. I'll see if I can find something to make you feel more comfortable." He went into Grandma's bedroom and found a duvet. He had almost reached the place where his grandmother was lying when there was a fresh fall from the roof. Walton was struck on the head by a roof tile, and fell to the floor.

CHAPTER 15

Help is on the way

About half an hour after Walton had embarked in Mr Hasenfratz's canoe, Mr Patel, together with his passengers Ollie and Nathan, arrived in his Volvo estate car at the place where the floodwater in Wainbridge met the road from Bristol.

"Gosh, what a mess!" commented Nathan as they surveyed the submerged or semi-submerged buildings. They could also see a few small boats here and there in the distance.

"That's the understatement of the century!" responded Ollie.

"Alright, maybe you'd prefer: What a scene of catastrophic devastation!"

"When you've finished practising to be a TV reporter Nathan, can you tell me whether you think you can find your grandma's house?" Mr Patel asked doubtfully.

"I think so. She's lived here since I was about six. I'll give it a good shot, anyway."

"OK, help me get the boat down."

As soon as they had untied Mr Patel's boat and lowered it off the roof of the car, he screwed the outboard motor into position, taking care to adjust the propeller a little above the level of the keel, and they headed towards the battered dwellings.

"I'll have to take it really slowly; it's like navigating around rocks at sea," said Mr Patel through gritted teeth as they drew closer to the small town.

"They say it's like this most of the time in Bangladesh," remarked Ollie, as his dad skirted round part of a caravan protruding out of the water at a grotesque angle. "I guess they're all gold-standard swimmers."

"Fancy a swim in this?" Nathan queried, as Mr Patel carefully steered the boat around a submerged Lotus Esprit.

"I might do so if I could claim that Lotus as my own!" Ollie replied.

In spite of the destruction all around, it was nevertheless possible to discern the basic layout of the roads, so Nathan was able to direct Ollie's dad appropriately.

"Ohh-h, Grandma's car — you can just see it all smashed up in what's left of the garage!" he groaned.

"But at least part of the house is still standing. Let's see how far we can get," said Mr Patel. He manoeuvred the metre-wide boat past the remains of the front entrance and into the house.

"There's a canoe!" exclaimed Nathan. "Someone seems to have come to help." Both he and Ollie began calling out: "Hall-o-o!" "Hallo Grandma!"

Instead of a helpful male voice that they were expecting, they heard a thin, frail voice saying: "I'm up here... is that you, Nathan?"

"Yes, it is! Hang on, Grandma, we'll be up there with you in two shakes!" And this was greeted by joyful barking, as Smudger recognised Nathan's voice.

Mr Patel had been retying the canoe to a lower banister spindle to avoid the travel bag getting tipped out into the water as it subsided, and now he tied his own boat likewise. "You go up first, Nathan," he said; "she's your grandma."

Nathan had no problem negotiating the staircase, and was soon in the guest room. Then he saw not only his beloved Grandma lying amid the wet rubble, but also his brother, who was not moving or showing any signs of life.

"Oh Grandma!" he exclaimed, looking from one to the other, "what's happened to Walton?"

"He was hit on the head by a tile from the roof," she explained weakly. "I don't know how bad he is — my leg may be broken. I've been trying not to move it."

Ollie now joined Nathan and they tried to revive the apparently lifeless boy. "Have you tried to find a pulse?" Ollie asked. When the older boy shook his head, Ollie grasped his friend's wrist and placed his fingers on the inner side. After a few moments he breathed a sigh of relief: "Ah-h-h, yes, I can just feel it. I wonder if there's any water anywhere that's drinkable."

"I'll see what the bathroom's like," said Nathan, heading in that direction as Mr Patel appeared in the doorway. He said hallo to Grandma, and went down on one knee beside the motionless boy. He ran his hand lightly over Walton's head. "There doesn't seem to be any external injury," he concluded. Seeing the duvet on the floor, on which the boy was partially lying, he brushed off a bit of the damp dust, and wrapped it completely around the inert boy.

"He went and got that duvet for *me*," said Grandma. "But I'm sure he needs it more than I do."

"Maybe I can find another," suggested Ollie. "D'you think I can find one in the other bedroom?"

"Probably; if you can open the cupboard doors. Watch where you're treading!"

Nathan found that the bathroom looked reasonably intact. The water that flowed from the tap into the beaker Grandma used for cleaning her teeth looked unaffected by the onslaught of the waves. He picked his way back to where the two casualties lay. "Let's see if we can persuade him to have a wee droppie," he said bracingly while Mr Patel propped Walton up, cradling him in his arms.

"Just hold it gently to his lips," he said, and they both tried to revive him for several minutes. But their efforts were in vain; there was no response.

"Well, he seems to have concussion, doesn't he," observed Grandma. "I wouldn't mind a drop of water, please."

"Why did you come in here, Grandma?" asked Nathan. "Why didn't you stay in your bedroom? It seems to be in much better shape than this."

"I did stay there for a long time, but then I needed to see if I could use the bathroom. When I came out I discovered that Smudger was in here. He'd got himself trapped under this bed, and I was trying to get him out when that beam fell on my leg."

"Is your leg broken, Mrs —?" Mr Patel queried.

"My name's Mrs Green, but please call me Loretta. I don't know whether it's broken. That joist from the roof fell on it, but Walton lifted it off," she replied as she sipped the water.

"Let's move it out of the way," said Ollie's dad, bending down to suit his actions to the words. "Ohh-h-ooh-hh! It weighs a ton!" He straightened up, leaving it in the same place, saying incredulously, "Loretta, are you seriously telling me Walton actually lifted that joist off your leg?!!"

Grandma replied with a soft smile, "He prayed for strength to lift it."

She had finished her drink when Ollie returned with the hoped-for duvet. He arranged it around her shoulders, for which she thanked him with a warm smile, adding, "You're Walton's friend Ollie, aren't you? I've seen you playing with him, especially when you were younger."

"Yes, we've been friends since primary school. Anyway, if your leg really is broken, we'll have to be careful about moving you."

"Well if it is, it's only my thigh bone — my femur. Maybe if Nathan can find an old sheet, it could be ripped up to make a bandage. Then it might not do too much harm to move me."

"Yes," Mr Patel agreed. "That sounds like a possibility. We certainly can't leave you here. But we also need some kind of splint — something like a long, thin, flat piece of wood..."

Nathan and Ollie stared at him, both screwing up their faces as they considered the impossibility of finding any such thing in the upper rooms of a residential house.

"How can we find anything like that up here?" Nathan remarked despondently, "like trying to find an ice cream in hell!"

"I'll have a look in the other bedroom," Ollie proposed, making his way cautiously in that direction.

"A couple of pillows wouldn't go amiss in the meantime," said Mr Patel. He followed Ollie into Grandma's bedroom and fetched two pillows from her bed. One he put under Walton's head, and used the other to prop up Grandma.

Nathan found an old sheet which his grandmother agreed could be ripped up, and Mr Patel proceeded to tear it into strips. When Ollie came back, admitting defeat in his search for a suitable splint, Mr Patel suggested the bathroom. "See if there are any loose shelves in any of the cupboards that might do," he added.

"Eureka!" shouted Ollie a few minutes later, as he returned brandishing a shelf that was about 30 cm long and 18 cm wide.

His dad took it and looked at it speculatively. "Yes," he decided, "I think that'll be OK, even though it's a bit wide. Nathan, if you can hold your grandma's leg with the splint, just high enough for me to get the bandage underneath, that would be helpful. Ollie, can you go down to the boat and get our first aid kit, please?" His son wasted no time in doing this while Mr Patel finished rolling up the makeshift bandage.

There was a roll of cotton wool in the first aid kit, which Mr Patel placed under the splint to cushion Mrs Green's leg. Nathan squatted down next to him, but his long legs seemed to be getting in the way.

"Come on, Nathan," said Mr Patel, "man up! You'll have to kneel down in the mushy rubble regardless of the effect on your jeans if you want to help your grandma!"

Looking sheepish, Nathan muttered, "OK," and went down onto his knees. He carefully lifted his grandma's leg a little, holding the splint in place.

Once her thigh was firmly bandaged, the next problem was how to transport them all back to the car, and from there to a hospital.

"The two patients will have to lie in my boat," Mr Patel suggested, "and one of us should paddle the canoe back to land. I wonder where Walton got it from."

Mrs Green responded: "He said something about a Mr er...something like Harzanfats, I think it was... I think he said he was the manager of a pub... the Ship and something..."

"I can paddle the canoe, Mr Patel," said Nathan, "we used to go canoeing on holiday."

"OK Nathan. If Ollie goes down into my boat first, we can hand him the pillows and Grandma's duvet, then you and I can help to get Grandma and Walton down into the boat, and you will be last to leave."

"What about Smudger?" said Nathan. "We can't leave him behind!"

"No, you can bring him in the canoe. Hopefully the owner won't mind," said Mr Patel. "Fold the side bench seats down, Ollie."

It was not an easy task. Nathan helped Mr Patel to carry his grandma part-way down the stairs, then he swung himself over. Grandma was then lifted over the banister, and was able to rest her right foot on the base of the banister. Nathan then found it possible to stand in the boat and lower her onto her duvet. "We made it!" he shouted exultantly.

Next came Walton's unconscious body; but although he was unable to cooperate, at least he was not as heavy as his grandma, so they succeeded in his case too, making him as comfortable as possible wrapped in the other duvet.

"Don't forget my travel bag," said Mrs Green. "It's on the chest of drawers in my bedroom." This was placed between the two patients near the stern.

Mr Patel moved his boat so that he could steady the canoe after Smudger was handed down over the banister, and Nathan was able to get into the canoe with the spaniel, talking to him in a reassuring way so that the well-trained dog accepted the situation.

"See you back at the car," said Mr Patel; "we may be a bit faster than you."

"Maybe — but don't bet on it!" Nathan challenged.

Mr Patel's boat was indeed faster, so he and Ollie set about transferring their patients to the car. The rear seats were folded down flat, and the resident travelling rug spread over the space available. Although Ollie wasn't tall, he was muscular, and stronger than the average 14-year-old, so he was able to help his father lift the casualties out of the boat and make them as comfortable as possible in the car.

When Nathan arrived, he wanted to know what they should do about returning the canoe to its owner. "We can't leave it here, can we," he remarked.

"Someone needs to stay here while we go and look for the pub and Mr Harzanfats," said Mr Patel. "Your grandma thinks it's probably up this road in one of the villages."

"OK, I don't mind staying here while you do your search. And Smudger probably won't mind too much either." Nathan pulled the canoe up onto the grass verge at the side of the road as the Volvo headed up the road in search of the "Ship and something". Smudger jumped out of the boat and frisked around, enjoying the long-awaited freedom of movement.

Mr Patel and Ollie had no trouble recognising the Ship and Shovel when it came into view at the first village they came to. Mr Hasenfratz was relieved to hear that his young friend's grandma had been rescued without being too seriously injured. And he was pleased to hear that his canoe was waiting to be collected down the road. "So where's the lad I lent it to?" he asked. They explained what had happened, and Ollie added, "We need to get them both to a hospital as soon as possible. Can you recommend one?"

"There's one at Taunton," Mr Hasenfratz replied, "or there's one at Yeovil."

"Thanks. But we've left Nathan, the lad's brother, with your canoe. D'you have any bed and breakfast accommodation available?"

"Well, not usually, but we can make an exception in this case. So I'll bring him back with me. Can I offer you some refreshment before you go looking for a hospital?"

"Well, we should get going, but a quick beer for me won't hold us up much. A Coke for you, Ollie?"

"Yes, please. I'm gasping for a drink," his son replied.

They bought several bottles of water, gave one to Grandma, and headed in the direction of Taunton.

CHAPTER 16

No room in the hotels

They decided to give Walton's true identity details to the triage nurse at Taunton hospital. She started to type in the name, then suddenly broke off, looking intently at Mr Patel. "The W-Wonder Boy?!!" she stammered excitedly.

"Yes. He was trying to rescue his grandmother from the tsunami when he was injured by a roof tile falling on his head. He hasn't regained consciousness since it happened. We don't know how serious it is."

A doctor examined Walton without delay, saying that his condition could be serious, but at least his skull was not fractured. "His bushy hair probably helped a bit to protect his head," he added, "but we can't say at this stage how serious the damage to his brain may be." His patient was allocated a bed in a side room. Grandma was made comfortable in a fracture ward while waiting for X-rays.

When Mr Patel and Ollie had said goodbye to Mrs Green till the following day, they looked for a hotel on Ollie's dad's smartphone. They all seemed to be booked up. "I suppose there's been an influx of refugees from up around the Bristol Channel," he commented. "Maybe if we try driving eastwards we may find something."

After several "fully booked" responses to their enquiries Mr Patel noticed that although the Talbot Inn was also fully booked, the car park was surrounded by trees and shrubs, making it unusually secluded. He looked at his son smiling speculatively, and saying, "I think we could get a reasonable night's sleep here in the car, don't you?"

"Yeah, why not? We've got Grandma Green's pillows and duvets to keep us snug as a bug in a rug!"

It wasn't the first time they had slept in the Volvo. Sometimes on holiday in various parts of Britain, including Scotland, Ollie and his dad had made themselves comfortable in the car while his mother and two sisters slept in a tent close by. It had been an interesting and pleasant change from the usual bed and breakfast.

"Shall we sleep in the front seats or in the back?" Nr Patel wondered.

As the back seats were still folded down his son opted for stretching out in the back. His dad rolled himself in one of the duvets, while Ollie lay on half his duvet, covering himself with the other half.

"Goodnight, sleep tight."

"Don't let the bugs bite!"

"Don't let anyone give you a fright!"

Next morning they were able to enjoy a good English breakfast in the Talbot Inn, both father and son having indeed had a very good night's sleep. Mr Patel found a discarded copy of the *UK Today* lying on one of the tables. As he picked it up he was shocked to see a headline across part of the front page: WONDER BOY INJURED — IN A COMA. But as he read on, he began to relax. The writer was urging readers to pray for Walton's recovery: "he prayed for others — now he needs your prayers". The report gave the location of the hospital as "somewhere in the UK". Most of the rest of the front page and most of the other pages were full of pictures and descriptions of the devastated towns around the Bristol Channel. Ilfracombe and Swansea, as well as Bristol, seemed to have suffered worst.

Walton was still in a coma when Mr Patel and Ollie were allowed in to see him. Ollie was taken aback to see tubes in his nose where he was receiving the basics to prevent dehydration. It was the first time he had seen anyone on a drip. He and his dad tried talking to him, but as before, there was no response.

"Well, we'll just have to hope that the prayers will be effective," said Mr Patel to Ollie as they made their way to the fracture ward to see Walton's grandma.

She was sitting in a chair with her leg in plaster. "Would you believe it!" she said with one of her dazzling smiles that proclaimed a DNA link with the schoolboy celebrity. "When they X-rayed my leg, they found that there was just a hairline fracture! They've put this plaster on to make sure the healing takes place without any risk of the bones getting dislodged. It's a miracle! You know how heavy that joist was, Mr Patel—"

"I certainly do! I agree it's a miracle that it's only a hairline fracture!" he replied in astonishment.

"I suppose Walton was praying for me on and off while he was on his way to Wainbridge. Did you find a decent hotel for the night?"

Ollie and his father gave her a description of their slightly unusual accommodation of the previous night, and Mr Patel wondered how soon she would also be needing somewhere to stay.

"I've been allowed to use a phone here in the ward," she said, "so I tried ringing my son Daniel, who lives near Exeter. I spoke to his wife, and she told me to let them know when

I would be allowed to leave here, and she or Daniel would come and collect me."

After taking Mrs Green in a wheelchair to the hospital cafeteria for some refreshments and more chat, Mr Patel and Ollie left the hospital. "We may as well check out some of the hotels near here — there may be some vacancies now," Ollie's dad remarked; "my phone will soon need recharging." They left the car in a car park near the town centre and walked around for about forty minutes. Eventually they found a small hotel with two single rooms available.

While Mr Patel went to bring the car into the hotel car park, Ollie put each of their mobiles on recharge in their respective rooms.

The *UK Today* was lying on the writing desk in his dad's room, and he settled down to read the harrowing stories. There were some amazing accounts of heroic rescues as well as heartbreaking disasters involving family members being lost to the waves. It was reported that the tsunami had been caused by an undersea earthquake about 120 miles west and somewhat south of Ireland. It had caused massive devastation around the coastal areas of southern Ireland, and considerable damage likewise on the southern coast of Iceland, as well as all around the Bristol Channel.

After a while he decided to see what was on the TV provided in their rooms. As he flicked through the channels he saw some more items of news relating to the tsunami. A minister wearing a clerical collar was telling the interviewer: "We took the advice emailed to us on Saturday afternoon by the Wonder Boy, Walton Dorsey. He suggested building up sandbags in a kind of molehill shape around our church if we thought it was worth protecting, and we had enough volunteers to do it before getting away in time. Some of us have been back there by boat, and although the water hasn't yet completely subsided, we could see that the sandbags really had helped — there wasn't much damage, and one particularly beautiful stained glass window was still intact! We're very grateful to the Wonder Boy for his warning and his advice." Ollie wondered which town or city he came from. There followed two similar reports from Newport and Weston-super-Mare, so Ollie speculated that the first might have been Bristol or Swansea.

A few moments later an Imam in Cardiff appeared on the screen, and Ollie could hardly believe what he was hearing. The Imam was saying almost exactly the same things as the clergyman, except that he was referring to his mosque rather than a church. He also finished by saying, "We're extremely grateful to Walton Dorsey for alerting us to the danger, and for giving us such good advice! Our mosque is not damaged much at all!"

When Ollie's dad returned, he was dumbfounded to hear how Walton had spent his Saturday afternoon sending emails to all the churches and mosques around the Bristol Channel. They concluded he must have done this while on a train. "Well, he certainly is a boy in a million!" Mr Patel commented admiringly.

The following morning they obtained a *Guardian* newspaper, and although most of the news continued to be about the tsunami, when they got to page 12, there were some different stories. There was a headline announcing: CHURCHES SAVED THROUGH WONDER BOY'S ADVICE, giving reports from Cardiff, Newport and Weston-super-Mare telling the stories of protecting the buildings with sandbags such as Ollie had seen and heard on television. Lower down on the same page were similar reports of mosques in some of those towns having been saved in the same way from serious damage.

Mr Patel and Ollie decided to spend a day or two exploring the countryside around Taunton and Exeter.

Merle O'Brien, meanwhile, had heard and seen all the news, including the stories of how many churches and some mosques had been saved from serious destruction through following Walton's advice. But the news dominating her thoughts was that her beloved was in a coma, and the doctors didn't know how serious his condition was. She could hardly wait for the Tuesday evening meeting at Kingsmount to start. She knew they would all be praying for Walton's recovery.

When Pastor Robnott appeared, entering through a side door, Merle got up from her seat near the front of the hall and approached him. "Hallo Mr Robnott, do you happen to know Walton Dorsey's parents?" she asked politely.

"Yes, I do. I've been spending time with them, praying."

"If they come this evening, could you tell them Walton's girlfriend has been saving some seats for them, please? You can see where I'm sitting — I'm going back there now. Thank you."

She returned to her seat next to two vacant ones bearing her bag and her jacket. After a few warm-up songs she was delighted to see Pastor Robnott directing a woman and a girl aged about 12 to those seats.

Mrs Dorsey spoke quietly, conscious of the possibility of someone trying to gather information about Walton's whereabouts being among the congregation. "I'm very pleased to meet you," she said, "and this is our daughter Esther."

The girl glanced at her mother, a little surprised. "But we've already met each other," she declared. "Don't you remember? Merle's mother took me with Grandma to see Walton at their house when her brother collected some of Walton's belongings."

"Oh yes, of course; I remember now. I suppose my thoughts were all concentrated on Walton at that time."

"Have you heard any news about your mother?" Merle asked as quietly as possible as the people gathered there began singing, following the words on an overhead screen.

Mrs Dorsey nodded and smiled her answer. While Nathan was staying at the Ship and Shovel, Mr Hasenfratz had allowed him to use his phone, so he had told her the wonderful news that her mother had been rescued and was safely in hospital in Taunton, with nothing worse than a possibly broken leg.

After the singing there were prayers for Walton Dorsey; for protection and for his recovery. And the "Amen" which followed rang out with a sound of heartfelt sincerity.

Pastor Robnott's talk was on self-control. As one of the fruits of the Holy Spirit, he pointed out that it came last in the apostle Paul's list, after love, joy, peace, patience, kindness, goodness, faithfulness and gentleness. He said that although this might seem to make it less significant than the others, it was nevertheless important for people to practise it on a daily basis. He went on to refer to the disastrous consequences that can follow as a result of people's failure to control their temper, or their language or their physical desires.

He had been speaking for about ten minutes when a young man came in through the side door, approached the pastor and spoke to him. It was obviously good news: Pastor Robnott's face lit up with a delighted smile, and he announced:

"We have just heard the news that the fatwa against Walton Dorsey has been revoked! The ayatollah who issued it has lifted this death sentence because he was so impressed by Walton's help to Muslims in giving them warning and advice which helped to save a number of mosques from being destroyed by the tsunami. Praise the Lord!"

Amid the shouts of "Amen!" and "Hallelujah!" Mrs Dorsey hugged first her daughter, then Merle as they shared their joy that Walton's life was no longer in danger from assassins. "What wonderful news!" exclaimed Merle exultantly. "We can go and visit him in hospital!"

Mrs Dorsey agreed, and invited Merle to go home with her and Esther so that they could make the appropriate arrangements.

On Wednesday Mr Patel and Ollie went back to the Ship and Shovel to find out how Nathan and Smudger were doing, and whether they could take Nathan back with them to Harlow. They enjoyed a really appetising lunch in the pub restaurant, and discovered that Nathan had enjoyed looking after Smudger and getting up late today and yesterday.

"What's the connection between a ship and a shovel?" he asked Ollie with a sidelong smirk and a wink at Mr Hasenfratz, as they all sat in the pub lounge later enjoying a drink.

Ollie pondered for a minute or two, then he replied with a mischievous grin, "If you spell the first word with a 't' instead of a 'p' I can think of a connection. You can use one to shovel up the other!"

Amid guffaws of laughter from the two adults, Nathan insisted that the first word had to be 'ship'.

Ollie tried again for a few more moments, then conceded: "I give up. What's the connection?"

CHAPTER 17

Teetering on the brink

With a grin still lurking around his eyes, Nathan explained: "The word 'ship' didn't have only the meaning of the modern word 'ship' when they first named this pub the 'Ship and Shovel'. It came from a German word 'Schippe' meaning 'shovel' brought over by the Anglo-Saxons. Probably the word 'ship' also existed at the time with its present meaning, so someone thought there was a bit of a joke involved."

"Well, I'm glad that mystery's solved," remarked Mr Patel, "I couldn't imagine what the connection was."

"My father came from Stuttgart," said Mr Hasenfratz, "and he said they still use the word 'Dreckschipp' ' meaning 'dustpan'."

When Mrs Dorsey, accompanied by Esther, Leo and Merle, arrived at Taunton hospital Wednesday afternoon they were told that Walton was still in a coma. The doctors were still concerned about how long he might live. However, they were allowed into the side room where he was still on the drip, but he seemed to be hardly breathing; there was no discernible rise and fall of his chest. Leo was shocked by his appearance, but managed to suppress any exclamation, letting his mother and Merle get close to the bed. Mrs Dorsey kissed her middle son gently, taking care not to dislodge the drip. "Hallo Walton, Mum here, so is Esther and Leo, and Merle is here as well."

His eyelids twitched slightly as she said the names of his visitors. His mother turned to Esther, "You can give him a kiss if you like."

The twelve-year-old approached the bed cautiously and gave her unconscious brother a little peck on the cheek, followed by Leo, who did the same, but whispered, "You've got concussion Walt. Time to wake up." This produced a slight reaction; Walton's head moved a little in the direction of Leo's voice.

Now it was Merle's turn. She bent over her beloved, pushing the tube aside, and gave him a tender kiss on the lips, followed by: "Hi Walton; Merle here. Have you heard that the fatwa against you has been cancelled? You can get back to living normally!"

Walton's eyelids flickered slightly, then fluttered, and a moment later his eyes opened. He looked around and sat up, saying, "Hi everyone!"

"Ohh Walton, you've come back to us!" his mother declared ecstatically. She darted forward, pushing past Merle, to hug her son, who had mixed feelings about "being back".

"I've had some wonderful dreams," he said enthusiastically. "I was in a really beautiful place, with amazing flowers with brilliant colours. And Jesus spent a lot of time with me, talking about all kinds of fascinating things. I didn't really want to come back." For a few moments his face wore a sad expression; then it brightened up, and he said, looking at Merle, "Did I hear you say the fatwa has been cancelled?"

They all assured him that it had. Esther explained: "The ayatollah changed his mind about you because you helped

Muslims to save some of their mosques from being destroyed by the tsunami."

"What about Grandma? Is she alright?"

"Yes. Nathan and Ollie and Ollie's dad rescued her, and she only had a probable fracture of her femur!" said his mother. "Nathan told me the news, including the fact that you lifted that heavy joist off Grandma's leg. That was a miracle!"

"And it was a miracle her leg wasn't badly broken," added Merle, "we now know that it was only a hairline fracture."

"You should write a book, Walton," said Esther, "with the title: 'The God of Miracles'."

Walton ran a hand through his hair and responded: "There's already a book with that title, written by Trevor Dearing and his wife Anne. The first section is full of letters thanking them for their part in the healing they received from Jesus."

They were denied further conversation as a nurse and a doctor came into the room, and the visitors were asked to leave. This gave them the opportunity to visit Grandma who was, of course, delighted to see them all, and gave them a first-hand account of her rescue.

Later that day Grandma was told that she could leave hospital as soon as transport could be arranged. So her daughter-in-law Louise promised to ferry her first to the Ship and Shovel to collect Smudger, then to their home at Ottery St Mary near Exeter to stay with them while her leg healed and her house was restored.

There had been a discussion at the pub-restaurant about returning Smudger to his owner, which culminated in an offer by Mr Hasenfratz to continue providing accommodation for Nathan and his grandma's dog until Uncle Daniel or his wife Louise brought Grandma with them to collect Smudger.

"Nathan is better than me at looking after Smudger, especially taking him out for walks," Mr Hasenfratz declared. At that point Mr Hasenfratz's telephone claimed his attention. It was Mrs Loretta Green, to say that she had been given the all-clear to leave the hospital, and her daughter-in-law would be bringing her to collect Smudger. "Would you like to speak to Nathan? I'll pass you over to him."

Nathan grabbed the receiver: "Grandma! Hi, how are you? Was your leg actually broken?"

"Yes, it was; but it was only a hairline fracture!"

"Gosh! In spite of that extra-heavy beam falling on it! That's a miracle!"

Grandma agreed that it was, and hoped to see him later that day. So the three visitors from Harlow waited for Grandma's arrival before saying a grateful farewell to Simon Hasenfratz.

Walton spent about half an hour trying to convince the doctors that he was well enough to go home. They considered that it might be dangerous to let him go without any medical treatment.

CHAPTER 18

No tears for Wonder Boy

Walton eventually agreed to let the medical staff carry out more tests, while he worked on restraining his frustration, and after another hour had passed, they finally conceded that they were unable to find any reason to keep him, and gave their permission for him to leave.

In a joyful reunion with Grandma he learned that Ollie and his dad had stayed in Taunton at least until the previous day, but she thought they were on their way back to Harlow.

"They had a lot of trouble finding accommodation in Taunton," she added. "They slept in the car on Sunday night."

Hearing this, Mrs Dorsey decided to drive back to Harlow that evening, although it would be very late by the time they arrived home. "At least we'll hopefully get a reasonably good night's sleep that way — maybe even a lie-in in the morning!"

Walton was delighted to have his travel bag returned to him, containing his mobile phone and tablet, still well wrapped up in their plastic bags.

"So, you were well prepared!" commented Esther as he unwrapped his mobile. "You learned that in the Boy Scouts, didn't you: 'Be Prepared' — a good motto."

But Walton was already engaged in texting Ollie. He then tried ringing Gareth. "Hi there, Gareth. Sorry it's been so long." "Oh! Walton! Great to hear you! Welcome back to the land of the living! Where are you right now?" "I'm in Taunton, but we're planning to come home this evening. I hope we can meet up tomorrow sometime." "Mr Goodman asked me to tell you he wants you to talk to the whole school tomorrow morning before lessons start." "Oh no! Not in the morning! We'll be late getting home tonight, so we're hoping to have a lie-in in the morning, if the media vultures don't pounce too early. Tell him I can do it after last lesson." "OK. See you tomorrow after school. Bye."

Ollie's texted reply informed him that he and his dad would soon be on their way home, and would be back in Harlow in the evening. It continued: "... I don't have much of an excuse for not going to school tomorrow. When can we meet up?"

Ollie was delighted to be told the news that Walton would be speaking to all the pupils of Passwords School tomorrow, so he was happy to leave most of his questions till then.

Leo, however, had been peering into the travel bag. "What's in that paper bag, Walt?" he enquired.

"Ohh! Grandma's present! I nearly forgot to give it to her!" Walton grabbed the bag, saying, "Thanks for reminding me, Leo," before presenting it to his grandma.

She was overjoyed to receive it. "Oh, it's beautiful!" she said ecstatically, spreading the headscarf out so that the patterns and colours could be appreciated. Her daughter and granddaughter agreed. "Yes, it's lovely!" said Esther.

"And to think of you buying it for me when you were in a public place and might have been recognised! Thank you, Walton!"

When the boy celebrity arrived at the school gates next afternoon at 3.30, he found Ollie and Gareth waiting for him. They slapped each other's hands in welcome, with simultaneous expressions of greeting, including: "What kept you?" "Don't make a habit of it!" and "Old friends are the best friends!"

"Thanks, Ollie," said the Wonder Boy, "for not letting anyone know where I was staying. And sorry, Gareth, for not letting you into the secret. I thought it best to minimize the number of people who knew."

"It's OK Walt," replied Gareth with a smile; "I did a lot of praying. I never did much of that before, but now I'm getting to be a pray-er!"

The pupils, most of whom had heard or seen the news of their star celebrity's recovery on TV or newspaper headlines such as: YOUR PRAYERS ANSWERED: WONDER BOY WAKES UP!, had been given the option of staying to hear what Walton had to say or going home. But about ninety percent had preferred to stay. As he walked towards where the head teacher, Mr Goodman, was standing at the microphone an ear-splitting, tumultuous clamour of cheering filled the hall. He waited for the frenzy to subside, then described what had happened, from the time of hearing about the fatwa while in Epping Forest with a friend. He did not, however, mention the gender of his friend. He guessed that the media people would harass Merle if they knew about their friendship, so the "friend" became a mystery.

His audience were fascinated by his experiences; many of them wishing they had been with him in Wainbridge to help. It seemed hard to believe that he had travelled down to the south-west of the country on his own, with danger lurking all around and waiting ahead of him. But most of them enjoyed the explanation of the name "Ship and Shovel", which he had heard from Nathan earlier that afternoon. When he had finished his talk and answered about a dozen questions, there was more cheering, including the singing of "For He's a Jolly Good Fellow", and as soon as he came down from the stage he was seized by some year eleven rugby players, who hoisted him up on their shoulders and carried him outside. The rest of the school rushed out to follow them, until there was a great, jubilant parade around the playground.

By Friday everything in the Dorsey household was back to normal, including the incessant phone calls and clamouring of reporters for their stories.

Walton cycled to 212 Latton Brook after the evening meal on Friday. The front door was opened by Mrs O'Brien, who became nearly as ecstatic at seeing him as his mother had been at his regaining consciousness. She gave him a hug that almost left him breathless before letting him come in. He couldn't disappear upstairs immediately with Merle, of course — her brother and father also wanted to express their delight at seeing him again and were consumed with the anticipation of hearing his story first hand. Eventually Walton got to the end of his account, and took the opportunity to express his thanks to the various members of the O'Brien family for all their help.

"I've got some biology homework to do," said Merle. "D'you know anything about the circulation of the blood, Walton?"

"Well, I know something about it. We were told to memorise the way it works, but I haven't had much chance to do so. But I can probably explain anything you don't really understand."

"OK, let's go up to my room and see what you can tell me."

When they came up for air after their long-awaited kiss, they stood for a few moments looking into each other's eyes, until Walton said, "Why don't we watch a movie? Can't you do your homework tomorrow?"

"That's a brilliant suggestion," replied Merle. "I'm glad you're human as well as superhuman!"

Jeff continued to attend the Tuesday evening meetings at Kingsmount Community Church, moved out of the flat he had been sharing with Cyril Cambit and in due course he came to know Jesus in a life-changing, personal way. His whole attitude to life was transformed, and as he attended the Sunday services there, he got to know a young woman whom he found most attractive. She reciprocated his feelings, leading to their wedding the following year.

When Jeff had read the report in *The World Today* of Walton's being carried shoulder-high around the playground, his reaction had been: "Someone should write a book with the title taken from that paper's headline:

600 CHEERS FOR WONDER BOY!"

Printed in the United States
By Bookmasters